LIAM

BACKSTAGE SERIES

DANI RENÉ

Copyright © 2016 by Dani René
eBook ISBN: 978-0-620-68507-8
Paperback ISN: 978-0-6398104-9-2

All rights reserved, including the right to reproduce this book or portions thereof in any form whatsoever.
The following story contains mature themes, strong language, and sexual situations. It is intended for adult readers.

No part of this book may be reproduced or transmitted in any form or by any means, electronic or mechanical, including photocopying, recording, or by any information storage and retrieval system, without permission in writing. If you would like to share this book with another person, please purchase an additional copy for each recipient. If you're reading this book and did not purchase it, or it was not purchased for your enjoyment only, then please purchase your own copy. Thank you for respecting the hard work of this author.

This book is a work of fiction. Names, characters, places, and incidents either are products of the author's imagination or are used fictitiously. Any resemblance to actual events or locales or persons, living or dead, is entirely coincidental.

The author acknowledges the trademarked status and trademark owners of various products referenced in the work of fiction, which have been used without permission. The publication/use of these trademarks is not authorized, associated with, or sponsored by the trademark owner.

DEDICATION

*To everyone who has ever walked away from
something, someone, or decided not to take a chance
on something they really want.
There should never be a time you don't feel good
enough.
You should never feel as if you're not worthy.
Whether it's love, a job, a dream you're working
toward, go for it, take a chance.
Do that THING that makes your heart full.
Because you are worthy, you should have everything
you dream of, anything that makes your heart smile.
No matter what your past is, leave it behind.
Look forward, that's where you'll find happiness.*

Our heartbeats, the rhythm
Our bodies, the song
Our love, the lyrics
And between lust & tears,
I'll love you forever

PROLOGUE

Two years earlier

What a fucking perfect night. The crowd was wild. My body is still buzzing from the adrenalin and the bottle of whiskey I finished. The two groupies who followed me back to the hotel room are playing on the bed. Leaning down, I grab the rolled-up hundred-dollar bill and inhale the thick, white powder on the mirror. One line. Two lines.

As soon as I straighten, my nerves alight with desire. An ache I need to satisfy. My cock is hard and thick, ready for a mouth, a cunt, anything they're willing to offer. I know my brother will give me grief tomorrow if this gets out, but who the fuck cares? I can do whatever the fuck I want.

"Lie back, beautiful. I want your legs open, wide. That tight little cunt is already glistening

for me." I stroke my cock slowly, watching the brunette recline on the silk sheets with her slender legs spread wide, offering me a delicious view. The innocent little redhead I found in the crowd tonight is also ready to play. She wants to please me—they all enjoy pleasing me. They're both smooth, shaven to the soft supple skin. Fuck, it's got me so hard. All I can think of is sinking into their tight little holes. I enjoy the perks my life offers up to me on a platter.

My brother doesn't understand why I love sharing. He never sees the point. But standing here watching these two sluts spread their thighs for me is a drug. It would be for any man. One that I will not deny myself. "Eat her. I want you to make her come all over your angelic face." Grabbing a second bottle of whiskey, I down a gulp. It burns a slow, methodical path down my gullet. Easing the pain in my heart and the ache from being alone. No matter how many women I have in my bed, ultimately, I am alone.

Watching the girls play has my balls tightening. Such a beautiful sight. Two willing groupies, wanting to make me feel good. For tonight, I will forget everything but them. The *brunette bucks and cries out as she finds release. My turn. "Both of you, on your backs." The giggles ripple over my skin as I watch them obey.*

Shaking my head, I lean in and slowly lap at the sweet, decadent treats on the bed. Both girls have their legs splayed and it's a buffet of honeyed pussy. I reach over and slowly stroke the brunette while my tongue feasts on the redhead. They're both dripping wet. Ready to do anything I want them to. My fingers plunge inside the brunette, and she moans. A low, sexy sound.

The redhead has her fingers fisted in my short hair, holding me against her smooth little hole. Her cunt is dripping. A sweet waterfall of honey, and I drink every drop.

My cock is painfully hard, and I need to be inside one of them. Straightening, I point to the brunette. "On your back, on the pillows." Then looking at the redhead. "On your knees. I want your face in her cunt." She doesn't question me, her movements fluid. I am so fucking high, flying above the pain that always wrenches me back to the dark loss.

Once they're in position, I sheath my cock, ready to plunge into the redhead. I don't know their names. Why do I need to? They don't mean much. They'll be gone tomorrow, and I'll go on to sell millions.

Yes, I'm a dick. I can have any woman riding my cock whenever I want. With a snap of my fingers, women drop to their knees. Why? Because I am Liam fucking Hayes.

LIAM

"Do not fuck this up, brother." Callum's glare hits me with a ferocity I have only ever seen on his face one other time. And that was when I drove him home from the hospital and helped Tay carry him into the house. My hand slipped and I touched her breast, which was an accident. *I swear*. He didn't think it was. My brother knows me all too well. How am I supposed to spend almost twenty-four/seven around her and not wonder what she would feel like around my dick? I would never do it, though. I love my brother and I respect Tayla too much to be an ass to her.

"I am not a child. I can handle being around Em without trying anything." I'm not sure if I am trying to convince him or myself.

"Liam, you can't fuck around with Emma. She's Tay's sister, and I do not want her crying into the wedding cake." With a groan, I turn to walk away, but he follows me. I knew he would. "You're not to kiss her, date her, fuck her, or *anything* her. Got it?"

Staring at my brother in frustration, I cross my arms and cock my head to the side. "Anything? So I can't pick her up from the airport?"

His blue eyes glare at me as he bites back, "Don't be an asshole."

Shrugging, I give him a smirk that I know will rile him up. "Okay, she's my kid sister, kind of. You happy now?" That thought makes me cringe. I definitely wasn't thinking of her as my kid sister when we were in London. She was definitely a naughty little kitten who loved to get her ass spanked while I fucked her. The memory of that night is seared into my mind. She came to the show to support her sister, and when I laid eyes on her, I knew I had to have her. She was different though, coming across as flirtatious but sweet. Not like most of our groupies who are pretty much fame whores. Emma is genuine, honest, and as insatiable as me.

"Yes, she is, Liam." Callum's words cut through my dirty thoughts, dragging me back to the present. With one last glare, he spins on his heel and walks out. He and Tayla are heading to Napa for a week before their wedding. I am supposed to babysit Emma. Well, not *babysit*. More like watch and not devour. The only problem is I remember what she feels like. What she tastes like. This is going to be one long fucking week.

I turn and make my way into the studio to find my best friend. He glances up, and I recognize the look on his face. He overheard everything. "Liam."

"Ryan," I return, flopping onto the sofa. I watch him work on the sound desk. Tayla is our sound engineer, but since she's off to marry my brother, we're taking a couple weeks off.

"I know what you're thinking." My brow creases into a frown, and I narrow my eyes. He knows exactly what goes on in my head on a daily basis. That's why we're so close.

"What am I thinking?" He's known me for ten years. He's been there through everything I've done, either telling me I'm wrong or giving me advice. I have made a few mistakes. Okay, maybe more than a few, but fuck it, I am trying to behave.

"Don't sleep with her." His warning will go unheeded; I know it deep in my gut. Emma had me gripped from the moment she stepped backstage. I can't explain it, but those alluring, brown eyes seemed to penetrate through my bullshit every time she glanced at me. Her smile lit up the entire arena. But it was her personality that hooked me, feisty and shy. That's a deadly combination. She told me what she wanted and how she wanted it, but when I took control, she allowed me to. Even though I'm known for my one-night stands, I wanted more than one night with her. I still do. That's why this whole situation is so fucked up, I'm going to be near her and I'm forbidden to touch her.

I lean back against the soft cushions, sighing in frustration. "I already slept with her in London, remember? She was hot, sexy, and sweet."

He stares at me for too long, and I know I'm going to get a lecture. "Liam, you know that you're a fuck 'em and leave 'em type of guy. Nothing wrong with it, but this is Tay's sister—"

"Goddammit, Ryan. I know who she is. Why the fuck does everyone keep reminding me?" My frustration is getting the better of me. I need to get out of here. "I'll see you later." Grabbing my helmet, I head toward the garage. A long ride on my girl will make me feel better. And before you go thinking that I'm talking about a girl with tits, I'm not. I am talking about the 750cc horsepower that is my Suzuki. The only woman who never lets me down.

The only thing my bike can't do for me is suck my cock. Turning the key, the engine roars to life and I pull out onto the road. Maybe a ride down to Santa Monica will ease the tension of the upcoming week.

Being alone with that feisty little minx is going to be difficult. Maybe I can convince her to stay at their house, and not mine. But if Tay and Cal find out I dumped her there, I will be in more shit than it's worth. I will just have to suck it up.

"So you're the famous Liam Hayes?" Her gaze lifts to mine and I can't help staring. The smooth, soft skin of her face is make-up free. Those long, dark lashes flutter seductively, and I bite back a groan.

"I am, you've obviously heard of me?" I question and am hypnotized with the way her tongue flicks out and wets her lips. They're shimmering and I find myself ravenous to devour her mouth.

"I have, you've got a big… reputation." The electricity swirling around us is at an all-time high, and the noise from the crew around us fades and I find myself under her spell.

"There's one big thing that you should be worried about and it's not my reputation, sweet thing." Her cheeks pink with a soft blush, and it makes her look even more beautiful. Never has a

woman disarmed me like this. I've never felt such an attraction, her body is fucking beautiful, but it's her smile that has beguiled me.

The memory is vivid, it feels as if it were yesterday, when in actuality it was almost six months ago. *I wonder what she sleeps in?* Something slinky, I bet. Those curves are going to kill me because I remember them like it was yesterday. The way my hands roamed over each and every one of them. That smooth, tanned skin that trembled under my touch. *Fuck!*

Opening up the engine, I speed down the highway, hoping to rid my mind of the images of that beautiful brunette. She's too young for me, anyway. She's only just turned twenty-five. I'm thirty-six. That makes me an old man in her book. *Doesn't it? I mean, would she even want me?*

She did in London. Maybe that was just for fun?

My head is already fucked up and she's not even here. The anticipation is killing me, and after spending six months at home, I feel as if I've been in lockup. I remember the time

I had with her—one night and two days—was enough for me to see that there was something between us. Who knows what she's been doing all this time. She might have a boyfriend. *Why the fuck do I care?*

Once I come to a stop in the parking space, I kill the engine and swing my leg over the bike. Kicking out the stand, I head into the dive bar on the corner. It's dead quiet out here tonight, just what I want. Normally this place is packed on a weekend, but in the week, it's dead quiet. A nice reprieve from the crowds. The bar staff normally doesn't give me the time of day, but as I step inside, the blonde behind the counter eyes me up and offers a bright smile. *Yeah, darling. I definitely came here for the view.* I can feel her gaze drinking me in. Every fucking inch. They're all the same.

Need. Want. Desire.

When they hear my name, or recognize me, it's even worse because they latch on to the idea of spending the night with someone famous.

My brother thinks I enjoy it. And, to a

certain extent, I do, but there are times when I want the fight. The chase.

"Hey, darling. Get me a beer, please?" Sliding into the stool, I watch her pert little ass sway in her tiny shorts. They're so short, I can practically see her cheeks.

"Here you go, handsome. What's a stud like you doing in here?" Recognition flits across those pretty eyes and I chuckle at her. Easy as pie. I could have her on her knees in no time.

"Just in need of something relaxing, babe. Why?"

"Well, if you wanted something to relax you, I'm sure I could make a plan." I stare at the bottle, the smell of hops invades my senses and my mouth waters. One taste. One small sip. It's all it would take to fall. To leap into oblivion and not remember anything.

No, I'm stronger. I don't have to drink it. I need something to take my mind off the drink sitting on the bar, perhaps those cock-sucking lips that look like they were made to swallow will do the trick.

I lock my gaze on hers for a second and

lower the bottle again. Her beautiful, shiny, blue eyes are sparkling with mischief, and my cock is ready to give her just that streak of rebellion that she's looking for by sinking into her mouth.

"Why don't you show me exactly what you have in mind then, gorgeous?" With a triumphant smile, she rounds the bar. I realize it's empty in here. She heads to the door and locks it. The sway in her hips has my dick hardening in my jeans. He's ready for some fun and so am I.

Turning on the stool, I face her. As she reaches me, she drops to her knees. Eyes the color of the ocean stare up at me, and her mouth curls into a warm smile. Rising from the chair, I undo my buckle. "Go on then, get that pretty little mouth working."

Her soft hands work my zipper. As soon as she fists my cock, a low groan rumbles deep in my chest. Her warm, wet mouth envelops the crown, and my head drops. "That's it, gorgeous. Take my fucking dick in your slutty mouth." Plump, pink lips wrap around me as she takes me deep, and as soon as my dick hits the back of her throat, I fist her hair, holding her still.

When I peer down, it's not the pretty blonde I see, but the brunette who is going to be in my house for the next five days. My hips buck, and the soft choking sounds spur me on. My orgasm has my body shuddering. "Take it, baby. Every fucking drop." Jets of hot cum shoot down her throat, and she swallows every drop. Slipping out of her, I tuck my dick back into my jeans and offer her a small wink.

She rises with a smirk on her pretty face. "You feeling better, handsome? Want to finish your beer?"

"Nah." I drop a twenty on the bar and make my way to the door. "See you 'round." Unlocking the door, I step outside and head to my bike.

My place needs a clean up before Monday. Knowing that I will have a beautiful woman in my apartment—one that I can't touch—is torture. At least she'll stay in the guest room so there's no chance of us bumping into each other in the bathroom. There would be no way in hell I wouldn't fuck her if I saw her wrapped in a towel.

She's a delicacy that I would love to indulge in every day of the week, but I can't. The road is quiet and I rev the engine, opening it up and speeding down the highway. The need to get to my quiet space is drilling into me.

My mind is completely fucked with thoughts of what just happened in that bar— it was a stupid mistake, but I did it anyway. It's what I do. My life has been chipped away by my choices, the severed connection I have with my emotions is beyond repair. I wreck everything I touch and everyone I come into contact with. The same way my father did.

Pulling up to my driveway, I hit the button on my remote and the gate glides open. Once the bike is safely tucked away, I head inside and the lights turn on automatically. I'm alone every night because being around my brother and Tayla makes the pain in my heart worse. They're so in love, it makes me cringe.

You may think I am an asshole, but seeing

people happy makes me angry. Pouring my customary whiskey, I stare at the glass for far too long.

My gaze rakes over the mess in the living room. The easiest thing would be for me to down the bottle of Scotch and forget life.

Turning on the sound system, I hear our newest song, the one I've been working on, blare through the speakers. Callum wrote it a couple of weeks ago, and I need to finish laying down the drums, but inspiration has evaded me. Who knows… Maybe my little peach will be my inspiration?

EMMA

"I can't believe you're going away and that I won't see you until the wedding." I know I'm whining, but there's a reason behind it. If they're not there, I'm going to have to spend five days with Liam. Alone. Yes, I would love to spend it with him, but we agreed that what happened in London, stayed in London. Although, a few days with him may be what we need to see if there is anything between us. Yes, we had a connection, but six months is a long time to get over that. I know I haven't. I still want him, I still think about him. Now I'll need to find out if I'm on his mind as much as he is on mine.

"You're not going to be alone, Ryan and Ki are here and you'll be staying at Liam's.

It's really not that bad, sis." She's right, I can do this. I am an adult who brought this on herself. Shit. *Did I have to fuck one of the hottest drummers in the world? Yes, I did. But did my sister have to go and marry his brother? Yes, I* suppose she loves him so I can't really fault her there.

"I'm *staying* with Liam?" I squeak my response. *Shit.*

"Yes, and about that...I'm not telling you what to do, but I want you to have your walls up. He can be an ass, but I have a feeling that maybe, just maybe, you may be able to knock some sense into him." I can't help smiling. My sister knows me too well. I'm as transparent as glass to her, she can see straight through me. That infuriating man is my weakness, and I would love to see if he's willing to change. If I can be the one to make him realize he's worth more than just a one-night stand. Or me for that matter.

"Fine, I'll be careful. See you in Napa, darling."

"Safe flight." I can almost hear the excitement in her voice. "And let me know when you've landed. I spoke to Mom and Dad. They're arriving on Friday, so you and Liam need to pick them up from the airport. And don't forget my dress." Grabbing my keys and purse, I get ready to head out to meet Margo for drinks. We studied together, and she's become like a sister over the past few years that I've been here.

"Okay, does he know all this? And your dress is already packed."

"Yes, I'm only telling you so you can remind him." The groan that escapes my lips doesn't go unnoticed. "Em…"

"Have a good trip, Tay. Say hi to Cal for me. Love you, sis."

"You too, babe. And please keep your heart locked away?" My teeth worry my lower lip. I don't want to answer that because, somehow, I know this is all going to backfire on me and I am going to end up falling for him. And my sister knows it, too. When I met him in London for their show at Wembley Arena, I was determined to get him to notice me. After they walked off stage and I came face-to-face with one of the world's best drummers, I was dumbfounded by him. Yes, he's handsome in photos and videos, but nothing can prepare you for seeing him in person. Caramel eyes, that boyish smirk, and those rugged features were enough for me to drop my panties. But, in the process of us spending the night together, and then the day after, something shifted. He didn't come across as the manwhore he's so well known for being, and it felt like we had something tangible between us.

Shaking my head to clear the thoughts invading my mind, I respond to my sister. "Go, have a good week, Mrs. Soon-to-Be-Hayes." Her giggle is soft, and I can tell she's nervous. Even though she's older than me, there's always been this serious side to her. I don't know what happened after I left, but she changed. Since she's been with Callum, there's been another shift. That's why I love my brother in-law, he treats her like a princess.

As soon as I hang up, anxiety hits me again. Opening my apartment door, I step out onto the landing and before I get a chance to lock up, my phone beeps. When I pull it from my purse, the name that flashes on the screen has my stomach flip-flopping and I can't stop the smile on my face.

* Peach, I'll pick you up at the airport, not sure if Tay called you. L. *

Seeing the nickname that he gave me that night sends excitement through my body. He still has a way of making me feel like a teenage girl with a crush. *Would I like something more than what he can give me?* Yes, I would.

I want what my sister has, something real. A tangible connection that can't be severed by groupies, or any other female, for that matter. Yes, the Hayes brothers are famous for their womanizing ways, but can't a tiger change his stripes?

As I walk the three blocks to the pub, I can't stop my thoughts from wandering to the badass drummer who made me scream his name in so many delicious ways.

Stepping into The Rose & Crown, my eyes do a sweep of the pub and I find my best friend sitting at a booth at the rear. "Hey, love."

"Oh my God, you're late and guess who was just here?" She's the most excitable person I have ever met, besides me. We graduated together at the Condé Nast College of Fashion & Design here in London, and while she's starting her internship in Paris, I start mine in L.A. I chose to go back to the U.S. to be near my sister, but I'm excited for the chance to intern with Katherine Kidd. Her designs are incredible, and the clothes she makes are modern, yet affordable. I would love to get an offer for a permanent position with her after my internship.

Scrunching my nose, I question, "That weird guy again?" I know exactly who she's talking about. She is adamant that I have a stalker, and I have a feeling she's right. He's been at the pub, my gym, and the store close to my apartment. I'm normally aware of him though, there's something intimidating about him and the way he always seems to stare at me.

"I'm telling you, there's something

strange about that one."

Ignoring the chill of fear that has goosebumps rising on my skin, I slide into the seat, grab the pint glass she ordered for me and take a long drink. I've gotten used to beer since I've been here, although it's not my favorite, but I'm not about to pass up a free drink.

"Yes, he's creepy, but he hasn't done anything or even said anything to me." Shrugging it off and pushing it to the back of my mind, we change the subject to one I know she's dying to talk about but I'm not. Liam.

"Are you looking forward to it? To seeing him?" Her question sends another wave of panic through me.

Am I?

"I don't know. He sent me a text and told me he's picking me up at the airport, but it was… I don't know, so formal. You know? Like… I mean we slept together. It seemed a little cold, to be honest."

Her expression changes as she considers what I've said. Sitting back, I wait for it.

Margo is strange that way. She'll overthink something before commenting, but she doesn't have days to give me advice this time. The last time was the morning after I slept with him, I called her to tell her he invited me to spend the day with him. She told me to go for it. That was definitely the best decision I made because I had an incredible day. Liam was attentive and fun to be around. We got to know each other and I realized he's never really dated a girl before, most of the tabloids show him with a girl once and never again. I've never seen him with a date, out doing normal things like visiting an amusement park or grabbing pizza at a small diner.

"Have you responded?" she questions, and I shake my head, handing her my phone. She scans the message diligently. "I think you should."

"What do I say?" I don't know why he makes me so nervous. Maybe it's the age difference; I don't want to come across as a silly little girl. I know I'm not, but he's a lot more mature and probably used to older women. *Would he even want me?*

"Love, you need to respond and let him know his chilly attitude doesn't bother you. Men love to chase, and you should let this bad boy do just that. You'll have him wrapped around your finger in no time." With a cheeky wink, she slides out of the booth. "I'm heading to the bar. What do you want to drink?" My last weekend in London, I might as well have another.

"Vodka and cranberry, please?" She scrunches her face at my choice.

"I don't know how you can drink that sweet stuff." Shrugging, I relax and grab my phone. Unlocking the screen, I open the message and hit reply.

* Just spoke to her, see you Monday. P. *

Hitting send, I stifle a giggle. "What did you say?" I meet my best friend's green eyes peering at me over the rim of her pint glass. I turn the screen to show her the message.

"Do I want to know why he calls you, Peach?"

"Probably not, you may be scarred for

life." We both burst into a fit of giggles. I know that if I ever have to explain why he calls me that I would turn crimson. The fact that he loved tasting me, telling me my skin was like biting into a juicy peach, he made reference to my ass while he gripped it when he had me bent over every surface of the hotel room.

"Right then, don't tell me. So, did you get that dress we saw for the wedding?" Nodding, I sip my sickly sweet drink and can't help shuddering.

"I did. I can't believe my sister trusted me to buy a dress of my choice. She's always worried about my taste in clothes, because I went through a few questionable phases. My emo goth was the funniest, and she hated it. But when I showed her my designs, she was pleasantly surprised that I've grown up and my tastes have changed."

"And you've finished her dress?"

"Yeah, I need to make final adjustments, but it's pretty much done. Napa is going to be amazing for the wedding. I can't wait for Liam to see my dress."

"Only because there's not much material to it." Shrugging, I glance at my phone as it lights up on the table between us. "Is that him?" Swiping the screen, I see his name pop up.

"Yeah." I drop my gaze to the message and I can't help grinning.

Looking forward to it, darling. *

The words send a rush of excitement straight to my belly. *Is he really looking forward to it? Or is he just saying that?* Before I have time to think about it, Margo snatches the phone from my hand. "Yes! I told you." At Margo's shit-eating grin proudly in place, I giggle at my best friend. "Babe, you know you want another ride on that stallion. Don't deny it." Her voice rises a tad too loud, and the couple next to us glance at me.

My cheeks burn with embarrassment. "God, woman. Can you keep it down? I don't want the whole city knowing I had sex with him."

"Just saying, babe."

"Yes, I do want him, but he's not

relationship material. You know this. You've seen the videos of him online. I mean he fucks everything with tits." As I whisper the words, I feel a stab of jealousy. He's gotten to me more than I would like to admit, and as scary as it is, I like him. Those caramel eyes, rough, calloused hands, and that monster... well, you know.

I can't fall for him. It's a bad idea.

"Love, do you really think I am that stupid?" Margo's thick English accent tears me away from my worrisome thoughts. She's right, I am fucked. Well and truly fucked.

"No, I didn't say you were. All I meant was that he's not going to be giving me a ring anytime soon. I would spoil his chances with all the groupies he gets to sleep with."

She reaches out and grips my hand, giving it a quick squeeze. "He's a man. If he thinks you want a ring, he's going to run. But, if he thinks you're having fun... that's another story. Then he'll want to give you a ring."

"I doubt one of the biggest manwhores will fall for me and give me a ring," I respond quietly. Even though I believe my words, there's a spark of hope in what my best friend says. Liam would have to give up his womanizing ways and show me that he can be happy with one woman. Me. My feelings for him are stronger than I want to admit, and I don't want to give in to his charms as soon as I land in LA; he'll need to work for it. And I'm going to enjoy challenging him.

"Callum did." She's right. We stare at each other for a little while before I shrug it off.

"I can't believe I am leaving in one day. I'll be back in LA on Monday and I won't see you for a while."

"Yeah, you big shot designer. Can't believe you landed that job with Katherine Kidd."

"Neither can I. My designs aren't as fluid as hers, but I want to learn everything I can. Who knows, maybe I'll be offered a job at one of the bigger fashion houses after. Now that would be incredible."

"Maybe you'll marry a stinking rich drummer, and he'll help you open your own fashion house." I pin her with an incredulous glare.

"Seriously, Margs?" Her lips quirk and she gives me a cheeky wink.

"Yes. You can have an amazing home with a picket fence and two point five children." Her comment has me choking on my drink.

"Who said anything about children? I am twenty-five, for God's sake."

"He's getting older, can't wait too long." This is what she's like, blatant to a fault. Most people can't handle her, but I love her sharp tongue. I can't find a comeback for that, so I finish my drink and slip out of my seat to get a refill. "Seriously, love."

Shaking my head, I walk up to the bartender who's leaning on the counter. "What can I get you, sweetheart?" He wipes his hands on a tea towel and offers me a sexy smile.

"Another vodka cranberry and a pint of lager, please?" With a quick nod, he heads off to pour the drinks.

"Can I buy those for you?" A deep

baritone startles me, and I turn to find steely gray eyes the same color as the cocktail shaker that sits on the shelf behind the bar.

"It's fine, I can handle this. Thank you anyway." Fear flows through me. Something about this man scares me. I didn't think he was still here after Margo mentioned him. My skin prickles with awareness, and I'm so glad that we're in public. The bartender places both drinks on the counter in front of me, but before I can pay him, the hand of the stranger darts out from beside me.

"I insist." He hands the money over and I can't help gawking at him. Margo is convinced he's following me, and I have noticed him around, but this is the first time he's spoken to me. His accent filters between English and American, and something about him has my hackles rising.

"Thank you. I have to go." Without a second look, I rush back to the table and slide into the bench seat. "That creep just walked up to the bar and spoke to me. I thought he'd left." I hiss, glaring at her.

"Oh God, what did you do?"

"I couldn't do much, he paid for our drinks." Her eyes widen, and I am sure they're going to pop out of their sockets.

"Did he put anything in them?"

"No, I held on to them. He just creeps me out." We nod in agreement and sip our drinks slowly. "Can we leave after this? I just want to go home."

"Yes, love, of course." Inhaling a deep breath to try calming myself, I gulp my drink faster. The sooner I can get out of here, the better. My phone buzzes, and as soon as I unlock the screen, a small smile plays on my lips. Once I've read the message, I lock my phone and drop it into my purse. I look back up to the bar, and my face falls when my eyes collide with steely gray ones staring at me.

LIAM

Flopping on my bed, I check my phone again. She hasn't responded. This girl has me by the balls, and we're not even in the same country, let alone in the same room. Laying back, I turn out the light and close my eyes. Hopefully I can get a good night's sleep. Tomorrow, Ryan and I are working on the track, and I need to focus.

"Peach, you look gorgeous on that bed." My words come out as a growl, and I don't even recognize my voice. Her face is ethereal. There's an innocence there that makes me want to corrupt her in the dirtiest ways. When she walked into the catering room tonight after the concert, I couldn't stop myself from hitting on her. I knew she was Tayla's sister, and she knew who I was.

That long, chestnut hair hanging in waves down her back, those beautiful chocolate eyes, and curves that can make even the strongest of men drop to their knees. She's incredible. Her beauty is unparalleled to any woman I have been with, and I know that tonight is going to be decadent. I can't keep her, I can't make her mine, but I can enjoy her while she's in my room.

"Are you just going to stare at me all night?" Her cheeky mouth makes me grin. Stalking toward her, I stop at the end of the bed, pulling off my tank top, and shuffling off my jeans and boxer briefs. I feel the heat of her gaze drinking me in. Every inch of my skin ignites as her eyes travel down until she reaches my hard cock.

When her lips part, a small gasp flutters from them, and I groan in agony. I am going to do things to her that will make her gasp some more, whimper and moan, and eventually scream my fucking name. I crawl up between her legs, my body hovering over her. Our mouths only inches apart, I can smell the sweetness of her perfume. Soft, sweet peaches.

"I want to savor you, darling. If we're only going to get one night, I want you to remember

me for the rest of your life."

Her hands trail over her bare breasts. Taut, pink nipples harden, and my mouth waters. There's only one thing I want to do, and that is devour every inch of her. My mouth finds hers — it's a soft kiss, but the hunger with which my tongue invades her is that of a man having his last meal.

I swallow the soft moan that escapes her lips. Happily. I finally break the kiss, moving down to her neck, kissing, nipping and licking. When I reach her pebbled buds, my mouth latches on, teasing, sucking. I graze my teeth over each one.

"Liam…" My name on her lips sends me into a primal overdrive, and the need to fuck her has my cock throbbing. Her hands fist in my hair as my tongue dips into her navel, and when I glance up, her body arches. Fuck, she's beautiful.

"Shhh, baby, just close your eyes and feel." Planting a soft kiss on her inner thigh, I suck the soft skin into my mouth. Without warning, I bite down, wanting to mark her. Wanting her to remember me tomorrow. Her hands tug on my hair, and the bite of pain has me groaning.

Her sweet scent of arousal is so intoxicating

that I know I haven't come across such perfection.
Ever.

"Please, Liam, just please?" Her begging whimpers have me smiling up at her. She peeks down, her teeth grazing her plump lower lip, biting down as my heated breath fans over her smooth, wet pussy. My thumbs tease the lips of her core, stroking up and down, and when I open her to my gaze, my heart thuds wildly in my chest.

"You're so fucking perfect." I don't even recognize my voice. Flattening my tongue, I lave at her sweet cunt. Again and again. Her hips buck against my face. She loses all control as she fucks my tongue, taking her pleasure, and it's the most erotic thing I have ever seen.

Her body is like a temple, and I want to worship every inch of it. As I slide two fingers inside her, the soft mewls that fall from her lips add fuel to the fire raging inside me. The ache to fuck her, to make her tighten around my cock, to feel her drip over me, it's about to incinerate me.

Pulling my fingers from her sopping wet pussy, I sit back and watch her eyes snap open. I lick her arousal as she stares at me. "I need you," she whimpers, her chest rising and falling with her rapid breaths, and I can't stop staring at her beauty.

"I know you do. Before I fuck you, I want you above me." I grip her hips and pull her up to straddle me. Her slick heat slides over my rigid cock, but I shake my head. "Not there, precious. Up here." I point to my face, and her eyes go wide.

"Liam."

"Now." My command sends a shiver over her, and she maneuvers her way up until her pussy is at my mouth. "Good girl. Now ride my tongue, baby. Fuck that sweetness on my mouth." Reaching up, I circle her clit with my thumb, and her hips buck wildly. Licking at her, I push my tongue inside her sweet tight hole.

"Oh, God…"

"That's me," I mumble on her sensitive flesh. Her hands grip the headboard above me, holding on, and I feel her pulse around my tongue. She's close, and I can't wait to drink every drop of her. My other hand grips her pert, peachy ass. She rolls her hips, lost in her pleasure, fucking my face, faster and faster.

When I reach for that forbidden hole between

her ass cheeks, she goes rigid, but the more I tease her clit, desire takes over and her body convulses. I slide my thumb over the tight entrance and squeeze her throbbing bud at the same time, sending her falling, tumbling, and screaming out my name.

Her sweet cum drips into my mouth, down my chin, and I swear to God, I haven't ever tasted anything sweeter than this. "You're a decadent little peach." The trembles that wrack her body subside, and her glassy gaze falls to me. My hands grip her hips, helping her shuffle down until her soaked pussy is once again rubbing against my dick.

"I have never done that before." she whispers, shyly. After what we just did, there's no room for being shy. Moving my hand between us, I grip my cock, positioning it at her entrance.

"Good, because there'll be a lot more firsts for us tonight." A cocky wink has her grinning as she slides down on my steel shaft. The heat of her envelopes me, and my eyes shut as I savor the incredible feel of her.

She's so fucking tight. Her soft hands on my chest have my body vibrating with lust. It's deep and primal, and I can't shake it. This girl is going to be the death of me. Her hips roll and the sensation is beyond belief. My labored breathing hitches as her cunt squeezes around me, as if she's trying to suck all the cum from my balls.

If that's what she wants, that's what she'll get. I roll us over and pin her to the bed. Her thighs wrap around my waist as I drive into her. My hips buck faster, filling her deeper and harder. Her head drops back and those beautiful chestnut waves fan the pillow, while her lips part in pleasure.

The sounds she makes have my inner animal unleashing all hell on her body as my mouth devours her nipples. Biting and tugging on the pebbled peaks. Our bodies thrum like the beat of my drums, and we move in sync, in a sensual dance that I haven't ever experienced. "You feel so fucking good around my dick, Peach. Let go, I want you to just feel me."

I fuck her deep, and her body tightens, pulsing. Her orgasm rips through her, and I feel my own following. Shooting down my spine, my balls tighten and I fill her deep with my cum. We hold on to each other, as if it's the last time we'll *ever be together, and the thought has my chest tightening.*

The alarm rips me from the dream. Sitting up, I hit the clock. It's six in the morning, and my mind and body are still shaking from the mind-blowing memory. "Fuck." I feel like a fucking teenager having wet dreams. Swinging my legs over the edge of the bed, I get up. I need a shower and I have to get rid of this hard-on.

As soon as I step under the spray, the hot water scalds my prickling skin. Fisting my shaft, I stroke it to the memory of my dream, to the images that play in my head. The feel of her beneath me, her moans, her hands, her lips. Every fucking inch of her driving me to abandon.

Memories of leaving her in London disappear while I jerk off to the idea of how many more ways I want to fuck her. Own every part of her. Possess her till she can't think straight.

My eyes shut as pleasure takes over. White flashes behind my lids, and I growl her name as my orgasm leaves me shuddering and shivering alone in my shower.

"Liam, are you ready for tomorrow?" Glancing at my best friend, I shrug nonchalantly, but I know he won't be fooled by my calm facade.

"Ryan, Liam, can I talk to you both?" Kierra walks into the studio dressed in a white sundress, and I notice my best friend's eyes light up. He needs to grow a pair and ask her out, or fuck her. They've been dancing around each other for years now, and the air crackles with sexual tension whenever they're in the same room.

"Sure, what's up?" I turn to the woman who is like my little sister. She's been with us for so long, I can't imagine what we would do without her around.

"I need to go home after the wedding. There're some things I need to sort out. I'll be around for about three days after we get back from Napa to finalize anything you need. My flight is booked for that Wednesday night."

I regard her a moment before responding. "What happened? Why don't you take the private jet?"

She shakes her head, and her lips purse into a tight line. Something is very wrong—she's never acted this emotional in front of us.

"Ki, babe, what's wrong?" Ryan rises and walks over to her, pulling her into a tight embrace. The emotion in the room is at an all-time high, and I feel like I'm invading their privacy.

When she pulls away, I can tell she's hiding something from us, but we can't force her to tell us if it's something personal.

"Are you sure you want to go to the wedding?" I ask. "If you need to leave sooner, I'm sure Cal and Tay will understand."

"Yes, I want to be at the wedding. I just needed to let you know I have to take time off after." With a small smile, she turns and walks out, leaving us in stunned silence. I cut a glance at Ryan and I can see he's warring with himself to go after her.

"Maybe you can fly out with her?" My suggestion has him spinning around to face me. Worry is etched all over his face, and I don't blame him. Ki is one of those strong-willed, feisty women. Nothing ever makes her cry. I don't think I've ever seen her shed a tear in the almost ten years I've known her. I need to talk to Cal. There must be something we can do to help her.

"Do you think she'd even want me there?"

"Bro, do you see the way she looks at you? You two are orbiting around each other, and it's time you make a play for her already. Because this sexual tension between you and her is going to start giving *me* blue balls." The comment earns me a scowl then a chuckle, because he knows I'm right.

"Fuck off, Liam."

"Ryan, I've known you both for years. Do you think I would tell you to do something that would hurt you? I love you both. You're like my family. I want you to be happy, and she deserves someone good in her life." I don't know where all this romantic, sappy shit is coming from, but the words spew out of my mouth before I can stop them.

"Then why don't you take your own advice, because you and Emma work. You looked happy in London, and when you got on the plane after the time you spent with her, you were a different person. So you need to stop being an ass and talk to her when she's here. Don't go and hurt her by using her."

"What makes you think I would do that?"

"I don't think you would do that. I can see how you feel. It's written all over your face. I can't wait to see how you're going to claim her because I can see you going all caveman and dragging her back to your lair." He guffaws at my incredulous stare. Something makes me think he's right. I know I am fucked. Well and truly fucked.

EMMA

Watching the sun bright in the early morning sky as the plane comes in to land, my nerves kick in as soon as the wheels hit the runway. In less than twenty minutes, I'm going to come face-to-face with him, and I have no idea what to expect.

I haven't heard from him since the message on Saturday night, and I haven't had the courage to respond. It wasn't something that warranted a reply, but I didn't know what to say even if I did. So, I just read it, over and over again.

As I disembark, I make my way to the arrivals. It's quiet this early in the morning, and my baggage claim is easier than I expected. Since I only have two suitcases, I can actually manage by myself. The thought of seeing Liam again has my stomach in knots.

I don't want to get hurt, and I know Tayla told me to be careful. To guard my heart. My sister knows me too well. I guess our fling in London was just that. A fling.

The doors slide open and I spot him in the crowd. He's in disguise, but I would recognize that lean, muscled frame, those incredible thighs, and that devilish smirk anywhere. When I near him, my voice drops to a whisper. "Hello, stranger."

He leans in and gives me a peck on the cheek. It's awkward, but his arm around me and lips on my cheek have me needy for more. My gaze drinks in the sexy man who's standing in the baggage claim waiting on me. Even under the dark hoodie, I can see his caramel eyes. Those same eyes that heat my blood and have my core tightening. The hungry way he stares at me has my body pulsing.

His dark brows shoot up in shock. "Stranger? It seems we need to get reacquainted." With a cheeky wink, he leans down and grabs my bags, and his spicy cologne intoxicates me causing a ripple of desire to coil deep in my stomach. It's been months and this man can still do things to me that make my body react.

"It's been a while. Didn't you forget me?" I question quietly. The curiosity in my voice is evident, and I hate that he makes me lose control so easily.

His gruff chuckle sends tingles down my spine. "I couldn't forget such a decadent peach, darling." His arm circles around my waist as we make our way to the car. Liam unlocks the door, opening it for me and I slip into the passenger seat of the luxury SUV and take a deep breath. The excitement of being home again is keeping me awake. Jetlag is a bitch, and to be honest, I just want to pass out in a comfy bed. Preferably Liam's.

He slips into the driver's seat and starts the engine. "So, where are we going?" My question comes out as a squeaky whisper. I was told—no, ordered—not to book a hotel. So I'm not sure where I'm staying.

"My house." My head snaps to him.

"What?" His gaze flits over to me then back to the road.

"I'm staying at your house?"

"Yeah, until the wedding when we're all heading to Napa. And after as well, unless you want to stay with Cal and Tay? They fuck like bunnies, so if you're happy to put up with that then go ahead."

"Ugh, no thank you." I giggle. My sister and Cal really can't keep their hands off each other. "I just didn't think I would be staying with you." The thought of staying with Liam is exciting. Even though we haven't spoken about what's happening between us. Uncertainty clouds my mind about the one night that will forever be etched in my mind, on my body, and subsequently, in my heart. Even though I don't want to admit it to anyone, I know my feelings for him are a lot stronger than I let on.

"Well, I have a guest room. You can stay as long as you want." His words are like ice water to my veins, and my heart rate plummets. *What did I expect? To move into his bedroom, into his life?* Shaking it off, I shrug my response.

"Yeah, sure. Sounds good." I plaster a smile on my face and turn to face the window. When he turns on the radio, my mind replays his words. Concentrating on the view, I take in the familiar scenery. Even though I have been gone for four years, everything looks the same. The Hollywood sign makes me sigh. I missed it here. Home.

Although I loved living in London, my heart was always back home. Tayla couldn't make my graduation, but my folks were there to see their baby finish school. Now that I have my degree, all I want to do is start my internship. When we pull up to a modern looking two-story apartment building, I gasp. There has been speculation about the homes the guys lived in, but I never expected this. The garden is vast and beautifully manicured. The upper level has a balcony, which wraps all the way around the second floor of the massive estate.

Liam pulls into the driveway, shutting off the car. Once he gets out, he rounds the front and opens my door, offering me a hand. The simple gesture has my mind running wild. I know I shouldn't let it get to me, but it does. I slide my hand in his, the rough, calloused hands that knew just how to make me whimper and feel so good.

With my luggage in hand, we make our way into the house. The interior is breathtaking. It's light, airy, and modern. White walls with gray and silver accents. There are two large black leather sofas in the living room with a glass coffee table on a bright red rug. A fireplace sits against one wall made of open brick, which looks out of place, but perfect at the same time. The muted shades are beautiful and understated. You would never guess it's the home of a rock star.

The large room opens to a modern kitchen with stainless steel appliances and a kitchen counter in the center. *The things we could do on there.* Shaking my head, I step farther into the living room and take in the breathtaking view of the ocean just beyond the patio.

"Come on, darling. You can get settled.

Are you hungry?"

"Yes, I haven't eaten since last night. I'm not a huge fan of in-flight dinners." The deep rumble of his laugh stirs something inside me, and I wonder if there is a possibility of us finding that easy-going friendship that sparked in London. We make our way down the hallway in silence, and I can't help noticing his jeans. They hug his thighs perfectly, and the way they sculpt his ass makes me want to grab it.

The bedroom Liam places my suitcases in is like a realtor's dream come true.

There is a king-sized bed, which looks as good as floating on a cloud. A built-in vanity sits to the left, and there is one wall of closet space. The window overlooks the ocean in the distance. Everything screams wealth, luxury, and escapism. It's as if I'm on vacation.

"This will be your room, so make yourself at home. I am going to get lunch ready. There's an en-suite bathroom if you want to take a shower first."

"Thank you, Liam. I appreciate this."

His chaste kiss on my forehead tells me all I need to know. All the flirting over the past six months has been pointless. He doesn't see me as an equal. I was fun for the moment, and now I am the little sister of his brother's fiancée.

That bothers me more than it should. Grabbing my suitcase, I unzip it, pulling out my clothes. Deciding on a pair of shorts and a tank top, I make my way into the bathroom. Black tiles and a shower big enough for two greet me. There is a spa tub in the corner, as well. *Too bad this bathroom won't be seeing any action.*

Turning on the shower, I strip down and drop my clothes in the hamper. Once the steam fills the bathroom, I step inside and instantly moan in pleasure as the warm spray eases my tired muscles. I hate long flights. This is a welcome reprieve after the trip. As the water cascades down my back, I close my eyes and savor it. Even though I am in the guest room, being in his house is strange. Does he see me as a little sister now? Or is there more?

I open the shampoo and lather my long, brown waves that fall to the middle of my back. Liam loved my long hair, fisting it while he took me hard from behind. Shaking my head of the dirty memories, I rinse my hair and body and step out of the shower. Maybe I should show him that I'm more than a girl. I can tease him until he can't take it anymore. Make him break. Wicked images flit through my mind when I think of all the ways I can tease him. With a smirk on my face, I moisturize my skin with the subtle peach lotion and get dressed. *This is going to be fun.*

As I enter the kitchen, I find Liam at the counter drinking coffee. His dark hair is tousled in that sexy, messy way he wears it. Like he's been running his fingers through it since he left me in the bedroom. A smile curls his perfect lips. "Did you have a good shower?"

"Yeah, that shower head is an orgasmic

experience." I giggle. His gaze darkens, and I notice the caramel is now a dark chocolate. Fuck, this man is beautiful.

"Really? And did you?"

"What?" My frown has him chuckling.

"Have an orgasmic experience?" My face heats, and I feel that heat spread over my cheeks and down my neck. I drop my gaze and turn away, and when I look back at him, he's watching me expectantly, awaiting my response.

"Liam, I never orgasm and tell." I turn to the counter and find a plate with a sandwich and a mug of coffee. Focusing on that instead, I grab my lunch and slip into the stool. I didn't realize how hungry I was until I sat down. Picking up the one half, I bring it to my lips and take a bite. It's utter perfection. The cheese is melted, and the bread is toasted just the way I like.

"Never? Well, I don't think you orgasmed in my shower. You're pretty loud, that much I remember." My gaze snaps up to his. His laugh echoes through the open-plan kitchen. Grabbing the kitchen towel, I can't help chucking it at him. Embarrassment flames my cheeks, and my stomach comes alive with the butterflies.

"Stop being an ass."

"Just saying, Peach. I remember you making sure the whole hotel knew my name in London." *Why is he talking about this?* I've been annexed to the guest room. He clearly doesn't want me. *So why recall the time we spent together in London?*

"Yeah, well that was a long time ago." Six months, two weeks and about ten hours to be exact. Not that I was keeping track of the last time I had the most incredible orgasm of my life.

"It was. I was—" The phone buzzing interrupts him. With a quick swipe, he answers the phone and leaves me in the kitchen. "What's up, doll?" The word rolls off his tongue like it's second nature, and jealousy rears its ugly head. It's my fault. I shouldn't have gotten invested. His reputation precedes him, and I should have known better.

Concentrating on my lunch, I take

another bite of the sandwich and finish it in a few bites. With a few long gulps, I finish the coffee, too. Grabbing the mug and plate, I make my way over to the sink. I am washing the cup when Liam rejoins me in the kitchen. He's so quiet, I don't notice him until I feel him behind me. His body is large, looming over me.

"Who was that?" I question, the words coming out as a whisper. He doesn't respond right away, but I can feel his hot breath on my neck.

"Nobody." He growls, but it's not the sexy, deep one I love, it's filled with frustration. I spin around and find his body inches from mine. He's close. Too close.

"Nobody called 'doll'?" I grip the edge of the sink behind me to keep from slapping him. Yes, I'm jealous. Should I be? Probably not, but that doesn't stop the anger slithering through me.

"It's an old friend." He shakes his head as if trying to rid it of a memory, and I wonder what kind of 'friend' he's talking about. He lifts his head and places a hand on either side of me, caging me in. "You want to do something fun, darling?" The change of subject is obvious I shouldn't be asking questions I don't want answers to . But his words are warm, and they wash over my skin like a soft blanket. Tingles race over my body. The tone of his voice is deep and rumbles like a sexy, purring engine, which has me clenching my thighs. Fuck, how can he disarm me so easily?

"Like what?" The words are a mere whisper, and the need in my voice has me cursing myself. He's so close, I can practically taste him. My eyes fall on his toned upper body. The black T-shirt hugs his chest and shoulders like it was painted on. The man has the body of a god. Sculpted, taut, and ripped in all the right places. My mind briefly flits to the memory of my tongue dipping in those ridges, dancing across those planes. What I wouldn't give to do that again.

His fingers reach up and lift my chin so that our eyes lock. He leans in, causing my breathing to hitch in my throat. This is the man who can make my knees wobble with a mere glance. "Anything you want." His voice is gravelly, vibrating through him and into me.

The spark between us is a force to be reckoned with, electrifying the air. Every inch of my skin prickles in awareness. He is way too close, and he smells way too good.

"Liam..." His name on my lips is a plea, but am I begging him to come closer or to move away? Should I force the issue and ask him about *doll*? I fleetingly recall my sister's advice and feel like I am already failing miserably at heeding her warning.

"I'm not supposed to do this, but I can't help it." His thumb swipes over my lower lip and my tongue darts out, following the path his touch ignited with heat.

He leans in closer, and his lips brush mine lightly. It's so soft and so sweet that I can't help reaching out and tangling my fingers in his soft hair and with a quick tug, his mouth is pressed against mine hungrily. He licks the seam of my lips, and I happily open to him, giving him a taste of me.

As soon as his tongue dances with mine,

a growl vibrates in his chest. His body is pressed against mine. The sink behind me presses into my back, but all I feel is Liam Hayes.

He swallows my moans and steals my breath, using it as his own. Like he needs mine to survive. His grip on my hips sears the skin beneath the flimsy material of my top. Our bodies are so close, it's as if we've become one person. Every soft inch of me yielding to every firm, ripped-as-hell muscle in his body. The feel of him has my core pulsing with need. The ache that I know only Liam could extinguish is alive and fighting its way through my body. But just as quickly as it began, he pulls away and spins on his heel, leaving me reeling from our heated kiss.

LIAM

Fuck! I shouldn't have kissed her, but God, she tastes so good. Sweet, delicate, and sinful. Slamming the bedroom door and inhaling a deep breath, I flop onto my bed and stare at the stark white ceiling. This is going to be the hardest fucking five days of my life. *Why does the universe want to torture me? Why do I have to be near the one person I can't have?*

A soft knock sounds at my door. "Um, Liam? I am going to take a walk." Her sweet voice filters through the door, and I jump up. In two long strides, I am at the door. When it swings open, the sight steals my breath. She's changed into a pair of yoga pants, and a white tank top that hugs every curve of her luscious body. Her gorgeous tits are on display to my hungry gaze. *Jesus fucking Christ!*

"Where are you going? You don't know the area. I'll come with you." When she shakes her head, I grind my teeth. *I did this.* "Emma, you're not going anywhere alone. So either you get over it, or you—"

"Liam, just fucking leave it, okay? You're not supposed to do this, remember?" she snaps, throwing my words from downstairs back in my face, and they cut me deep. *Why am I such a dickhead?* I take a step toward her, which has her stepping back, turning, and sprinting down the hallway. She heads into the guest room and shuts the door with a loud slam. I deserved that.

I take tentative steps toward her room and lift my hand to knock on the door. Her sniffles from the other side gut me. Inhaling a deep breath, I knock. It's quiet for such a long while that I think she's ignoring me. Then the door cracks, and big doe eyes peer up at me. "What?"

"Can we talk?" She stares at me, then nods. Stepping back and pulling the door wider, she allows me entry. As soon as I walk into the room, my senses are assaulted by her peach-scented perfume, lotion, whatever the fuck it is, and my dick throbs behind my zipper. A quick glance shows me she's unpacked her two suitcases, but not into the closet. All her clothes are on the bed. My gaze falls on a pair of red lace panties, and I am now so fucking hard, I would give a steel pipe a run for its money. My desire to drive into her tight cunt is rendering me speechless.

"Talk, Liam. I don't know what you have to say, but do it quickly. I want to unpack and go out." Turning to face her, I take in the woman I'm desparate to touch. She's so beautiful, so perfect, but I'm no good for her. There's no way I can give her a forever. I can't promise her that I am a good person, because I'm not.

"Peach, I'm trying to do the right thing here. I need you to understand that I'm not right for you. We had an incredible time together, but you deserve someone decent."

Her eyes narrow and an adorable crinkle

forms in the center of her brow. Like she can see right through my bullshit. "Yeah, you mean someone who isn't going to fuck the next random chick who catches his eye?" Her question grates through me. Lifting my gaze to meet hers, I see the determination in her beautiful chocolate eyes. She's hardened herself to me, and it hurts, but it's good.

"Yes." There's nothing more to say. Her answering nod confirms she understands where we stand. Then she crosses her arms in front of her, and her tits push up in the tiny tank top. I'm sure I am going to come in my fucking jeans if I don't get away from her in the next two seconds.

"Fine. Great talk. You can leave now." *She's kicking me out of my own house? Well, room?* Fuck, I would love to punish her peachy little ass right now. I head to the door but glance back at her. There's a hardness to her stance, but her trembling hands don't escape my notice. She's as affected by me as I am by her. Without another word, I walk out, leaving her fuming. It's better she hate me than want me. It will make it easier for her to get over whatever we had.

Back in my bedroom, I grab my phone and type out a message to someone I know will take the edge off. I shouldn't, but I can't stop. I want Emma, and I can't have her. The reply comes instantly. Grabbing my jacket and helmet, I make my way out to the living room. The door of the guest room is shut, so I leave a note on the table with the keys to my car.

In no time, I'm on the highway heading toward a place I haven't been to in a while. To a woman I have on speed dial if I need her.

When I pull up to the apartment, her door opens. She's standing there in a pair of yoga pants that mold to her beautiful, toned thighs. Her tiny scrap of a top doesn't leave much to the imagination. The same outfit on the girl I just walked out on had me hardening in seconds, but she's not Emma.

"Liam Hayes, it's been a long time. Come in." Her apartment is luxurious. It's obvious a woman lives here. Everything is *pretty*.

"It has been, darling."

"To what do I owe the pleasure? Is it the girl from London you told me about?"

"Mo, can we not talk about that?" Monique is a longtime friend of over a decade. She's been around the block with me, knows my deepest, darkest demons, and she is still here. The only thing I give her now is my secrets. I haven't fucked her in a long time. But that doesn't stop her from trying.

She's pulled me—no, dragged me—from the gutter more times than I can count. Almost as many times as my brother and Ryan have.

"She's doing a number on you, bad boy," she states with a hand propped on her hip. I follow her into the spacious living room. That black leather sofa has seen more action than my whole apartment. I met Monique when she was a stripper. She was in school and trying to put herself through college. What a cliché life can be. The filthy, bad boy rock star and the equally-as-bad stripper.

"I need her but I can't have her." The growl in my voice has a shiver running over her body. When I glance at her, there's nothing about her that reminds me of Emma. There's no reason for me to even think about her, because when I do, that foreign feeling— that ache in my chest—becomes unbearable.

"Do you want to fuck me? Pretend I'm her?" She pushes down her yoga pants, over her curvy thighs, revealing her bare flesh that's begging for me. Aching. Dripping. Needing. She's always ready.

I turn away and look at the beach in the distance. "You love this, don't you? Is that why you stick around?" I gesture between us. She's standing there half-naked, but I feel nothing.

I know my words cut her, hurt her, but I can't bring myself to take them back. I don't allow any emotion to play a role in my life. And that's okay by me, because that means I don't get hurt.

"Mo, answer me. You of all people know I can't give someone forever. Fucking answer me!" I am shaking with anger.

"Yes, yes, Liam. That's why I stick around." She pulls her pants up and when she's fully dressed, she flops onto the sofa.

I don't want this.

I want what my brother has.

I want love.

The realization hits me so deep that my breathing stops. When Monique turns to me, her face falls. "Are you in love with her?" It's too soon. We barely know each other. She's someone I *could* love, but I know fuck all on the *how* part. "Stop telling yourself you don't. You're too fucking scared to feel anything because you wonder if you'll turn out like your father. I know that's the reason. You can't lie to me. I'm here to tell you that you won't. You're stronger."

Pushing up from her sofa, she leaves me in her living room, stunned and deafened by my heartbeat hammering in my ears. I lean back and close my eyes. My father, the fuck-up.

It's been a while since I thought about him, but the fear of turning out like him is always there. Just beneath the surface. Slowly beating away at me. Chipping away at the tiny cracks that I made when I was young and foolish.

I know if it weren't for my brother, I would probably be six feet under by now. And if it weren't for Mo, I would be living in a trailer. And as for Ryan, fuck, he's put up with so much shit from me. I'm lucky. I know that. But deep down, I am still empty. I am still a shell of a man.

Desolate.

Cold.

Heartless.

"Do you want to go to a meeting? Maybe we should. I will go with you. Drink this." She hands me a glass of water. I peer up and find her kind, emerald eyes watching me. Waiting for my reaction.

"Thanks." Grabbing the water, I gulp it down in two long pulls. "I almost had a beer."

"One beer wouldn't have killed you. Stop being such a pussy. You're strong. You've been through more than most people endure in their entire lifetime. If this girl means so much to you already, then why don't you take a chance with her?"

"My brother asked me to steer clear of her. I'm still in recovery. I can't be in a relationship." I cut a glance to her and find her staring at the ocean, which is just a block away from her apartment. You can see water for miles out here. That's something I love about my home—I can sit and watch the waves crashing on the shore for hours.

"I don't believe in that shit. We both stopped at the same time. If you're strong enough to walk away from a drink, then you're just like a regular man."

I chuckle, but it's humorless. "Can I ever be a regular man?" The question is more for myself, but I don't know if I can ever answer that. Setting the glass down, I turn to her. She's got her gaze trained on me, watching my every move.

"Yes, you are. Don't you see that? You need to stop living in your past. What you did then isn't what you're doing now. Everyone has done shit in their lives—it's what you're doing in the present and what you want in your future." Her soft sigh makes me crumble. "I'm sorry about earlier.

You've always come to me for... release."

"It's fine. Appreciate you for putting up with me being a dick." There's nothing more I want than to have a normal life. To have a wife, kids, maybe even a dog. My mother would be so proud. I can't help but chuckle at that.

"What?"

"Just thinking. Like to have a dog one day." When I look back at Mo, she's staring at me like I've gone insane. Maybe I have. "My mother and her dogs," I say by way of explanation.

"Ah yes, the dogs." Since my mother is an advocate for the animal shelters in LA, we always tease her and tell her she's going to end up with a farmyard of animals. Which I know she'd be fine with. "Liam, do you trust me?"

I nod, meeting her intense stare, and I know I am in for a lecture.

"You're going to be okay. Being with someone... You never know. She might be the one who cracks the whip and sets you straight. The one who will make you see sense, and you'll end up putting a ring on it." She sings those last few words in tune with the song and that has me barking out a laugh.

Part of me would love just that, but before I do anything, I need to make sure I'm there. That I have the strength. I decide to take this week and test my strength in being *'normal.'*

EMMA

Liam Hayes is such an asshole. I stare at the note he left on the table. Probably gone out to fuck some random woman. That's what he does. I'd by lying if I said it didn't hurt. When he rejected me earlier, it took all my strength not to break down in tears, but I refuse to give him that satisfaction.

Making my way into the kitchen, I open the fridge and find ingredients for a bolognaise. I am starving again, so I start the sauce and put the pasta on to boil. Turning on some music, I notch up the volume until all I hear is Callum Hayes singing about Love & Fire. It's a song he wrote for Tayla when they broke up. It's so beautiful. His love for her bleeds through the lyrics.

Completely. Unbidden. Irrevocably.

I want that for myself.

Lifting the pot from the heat, I drain the water and scoop the pasta into a large bowl. I add in the tomato and coriander sauce. The aroma fills the kitchen and ultimately the living room, as well.

As soon as I am comfortable on the plush sofa, the door flies open and Liam stalks in. The look on his face is indifferent. His eyes flit between the kitchen and me. I didn't realize he'd be back so soon, so I'm only wearing an old college T-shirt and a pair of panties. My bare legs are curled under me on the sofa.

"You cooked." It isn't a question, more like an accusation. I nod, my throat suddenly thick with fear that I have pushed my houseguest boundaries too far. Our eyes lock in what can only be described as a heated stare-down. There's an undeniable emotion in his gaze, but it disappears instantly. "Thanks." He turns and walks into the kitchen, pulling out a plate and cutlery. How the fuck can he walk in here and act like nothing is wrong?

I watch him shift around the empty space, the muscles in his shirt bulging and tightening as he moves. He isn't huge, as in bulky, but there is definition in his arms and shoulders that reminds me of what those muscles looked like towering over me. *God, this is ridiculous.* I'm supposed to be angry with him. Narrowing my eyes, I shoot daggers his way, but of course, he doesn't notice because he's not even looking at me.

Once he's plated some dinner, he walks over to the sofa and sits down next to me. He casts a glance at the television, which I had turned on since I thought I'd be dining alone. His dark hair is messy. He probably just pulled off his helmet. His jaw is dusted with a light stubble that contours his chiseled features and has me aching to run my hands over it.

"Is it okay?" I gesture to the plate. Hazel eyes pin me to the sofa as he slowly takes in my appearance.

"It's incredible, Peach. Didn't know you could cook. I may keep you around longer." He offers me a cheeky wink, and my insides turn to molten lava. *Why does he do that? Act like we're dating or living together in one breath and then turn a cold shoulder in the next.*

"Don't want to mess up your chances at a one-night stand." Dropping my feet to the plush white rug, I rise and walk to the kitchen. I can feel his gaze on me. It sears my skin and sends a rush over my body.

Suddenly, I feel him behind me, and when my plate hits the sink, I am spun around. Big hands grip my hips and the fire in his eyes scorches me as his body presses me into the counter. I can feel the ridge of his erection digging into my stomach. *Fuck, I want to slap him and kiss him.*

"Why do you always like to fuck with my head, Peach?" His voice is low and gravelly.

"What? I didn't do anything." His breathing is ragged and fans over my face, our lips inches apart. His heat is unbearable. His fingers press into my hips, holding me steady, but I feel delirious being so close to him and not being able to touch him. Or kiss him.

"This. Isn't. Happening." The harsh reminder of his rejection slices me open. Flaying me to his intense gaze. My heart constricts in my chest, and the lump in my throat chokes me. Placing both hands on his chest, I push him away, and he lets me.

"I didn't ask to be here. I don't fucking want you to do something you'll clearly regret. So why don't you take me to a fucking hotel. Because I can't deal with this shit." My voice raises to a screech. "You're an asshole. Just leave me the fuck alone."

I storm past him and he reaches for me. "Em—" I jerk away from his grasp and make my way to the bedroom. Once there, I tug on a skirt, grab my purse, and head into the hallway where I find car keys waiting for me. I expect him to stop me from leaving, but when he doesn't, I walk out without a backward glance.

As soon as I am in the car, I let out a breath I didn't realize I was holding. How can I be so hurt by someone who doesn't give a shit about me? I need to get a hold of my feelings. Liam's presence in my life isn't going anywhere. We're meant to spend the week together, though I don't think I can. Once the anger boiling inside me is at a low simmer, I pull out of the garage and head down to Santa Monica. The beach will be quiet since it's late, so I can just sit quietly and listen to the waves crashing.

There is no way I can let Tay know that I'm harboring such strong feelings for him. She warned me. She fucking told me. And here I am about to burst into tears because I didn't listen to her.

Pulling into a parking spot, I turn off the engine and the tears that I've been holding back spill. I grab my purse and open the door. I need fresh air. Maybe a walk would do me good. Once the alarm on the car locks the doors, I make my way down to the pier. I was right; it's quiet down here. There are a few couples walking along the beach, but other than that I am on my own. As usual.

At twenty-five, I didn't think it would be possible to feel so alone. I have friends, my sister, but I know that the missing part of me is my heart. It's empty. Since that fateful night in London, I've tried to fill it with meaningless flings, but it's been pointless. There seems to be one man who's been on my mind since we met six months ago. The only man I can't have.

He's so closed off to any feelings now that he pushes me away, and I know that there's something more between us. He was so attentive and caring taking me out on a date before they left London. Even though it was one day, I *felt* his emotions. Perhaps that's why it hurts. He let me in once, but somehow, since I landed in L.A., the walls have come up and there's nothing there. Just the shell of a man with too many women and not enough time. That thought stings.

The cool air is calming, and as the breeze picks up, a shiver runs over my body. "You shouldn't be out here alone." The deep timbre of a familiar voice has me pivoting. Even in the dark, his heated stare holds me hostage. There's no one else on the pier, just me and him. He stalks toward me like a predator hunting his prey.

"Why do you care? Oh right, because I

am your little sister. Isn't that right, Liam?"

"Emma." The warning in his tone is unmistakable.

"You may not know this, but I am a grown woman, and I can go wherever I want whenever I want." My grip tightens on the strap of my bag, and the hold I have on the car keys turns my knuckles white.

We're in a standoff, and the only thing stopping anything from happening is Liam. The wall that's built around him is so high, I doubt I will ever be able to climb it. Let alone break it down. *Do I just wait around for him? No, I deserve more.*

"Do not talk to me like that. You're under my care. I suggest you act like an adult if you want to be treated like one. Running out on me is not what a grown-up would do."

Anger flares in my chest. If he were standing any closer, I would have slapped him. That was a dick thing to say. "Fuck you, Liam."

"If I remember correctly, we already have."

"Why do you have to be such an asshole?

Do you get off on it? Do you enjoy hurting people who care about you?" My tirade stops when he closes the gap between us, his body caging me in between his arms and against the wooden beam of the pier.

When he leans in, my breath quickens and my pulse riots. Even though I'm enraged with him, I want to feel his lips on mine. If he kisses me, I know we'll end up in his bed. There's no doubt about that. *Do I want that?* To be another notch on his bedpost, again? Yes, for the life of me, as bad as it sounds, I want it. I want him. "Why are you being this way?" I ask quietly.

"I'm being this way to make you stop looking at me like that." His growl is feral, and I want him between my legs, showing me exactly what an animal he can be. I am his prey, after all.

"Like what?" My words are breathy, filled with yearning. My heart races in my chest, but when Liam leans in farther and presses his lips to my ear, my body turns to liquid.

"Like you want me to take you..." His

tongue slowly traces a wet, hot trail along the shell of my ear. "… bend you over my bike …" His teeth graze the lobe, biting down softly, eliciting a whimper from my lips. "… hike up your short skirt, tug your tiny panties off, then fuck you into oblivion." Every word ignites a fire so deep in my core that I don't think it will ever be extinguished. His teeth sink into my earlobe again, this time harder, tugging it, sending pleasure straight to my clit.

My nerves are frayed, and I am trembling with unadulterated lust. I squeeze my thighs together, trying to calm the ache, but it's no use. There's only one thing that will sate me, and he's standing in front of me.

LIAM

I'm so close to her. The scent of her perfume engulfs my senses, and I know there's no turning back. The exquisite feel of her body against mine is too much. My cock throbs behind the zipper of my jeans. When she walked out of my house, I followed her. To find her standing alone in the dark angered me, and now all I can think about is spanking her peachy ass.

"Emma, you need to get in that fucking car and drive back to my house. Now. I'll be right behind you."

"What makes you think you can order me around?" Her sassy little mouth and that indignant tone only spur me on. She's trying to make me angry, but all she's doing is turning me the fuck on.

"Peach, do not make me tell you again." There is a warning in my words, but when she folds her arms across her chest, lifts her chin and glares at me, I have to stifle a chuckle. *She's so fucking adorable.*

"What are you going to do, spank me?"

Fuck, yes, I would love to do that. "Sweet cheeks, don't fucking tempt me. Trust me, I am definitely not averse to putting you across my knee." Even in the dark, I can see the pink dusting her cheeks. She drops her head and eyes the space between us.

Reaching up, I lift her chin with my index finger so her eyes are on me. I don't know why, but I want them piercing me. She makes me accountable for my mistakes, my transgressions. This woman makes me want to be a better man. "Please?"

I have never begged a woman for anything. I have never pleaded like I do with her. She's slowly unravelling me. The persona I have built over the years is crumbling, and I don't know how to stop it. I don't know if I want to stop it. I would give up the fame just to see a smile on her face and to see her eyes sparkle with amusement. To hear her giggle.

When she nods and walks past me, it takes every bit of my restraint not to grab her, press her against the barrier and fuck her senseless. But I promised my brother. I can't hurt her.

She moves past me, and I hear the soft footfalls of her walking away from me. Rubbing my hand over my face, I glance back and realize she's already in the car. I hear the engine start, but she doesn't pull away.

I make my way up to the bike, swing a leg over, and slide on my helmet. I peer at the car, waiting for her to pull away, but she's just sitting there. Turning to me, she offers a small smile, one that doesn't reach her eyes and I know I've fucked up. Not even two days into having her here, and she's already in tears. *Jesus, I am such a fuck up.* I'm trying to do the right thing, and I can't even get that right.

How am I going to fix this? I need to. Hurting her wasn't my intention. As I watch her pull away, my heart thuds with anxiety. As the car disappears down the road, I turn the key and my girl roars to life between my legs. Fuck, I love that feeling. If only it was Emma between my legs.

I follow her all the way back to the house, my mind swirling with thoughts of her.

What can I give her to make this right? Is there even a possibility that I could give her a forever right now? Am I the marrying kind? I can't answer that, yet, but I can try to give her a week and if she still wants me after, then I'll have to work at it.

Moments later, I'm behind her on the highway. She's a careful driver, but I am dying to get her home. I don't know what I'm going to do, but she's going to fucking talk to me. We need to do something about this tension between us. I can't deal with it.

Fifteen minutes later, we're parking in the garage. As I pull my helmet off, I catch a glimpse of her bare legs walking up to the house. She's not said a word. She didn't even wait for me to walk her in. I suppose she is my guest and I want her to feel comfortable in my home.

Walking up to the front door, I push inside since she left it cracked for me.

The vision of her standing there with her eyes shining has my heart rate speeding up. Emma is staring up at me with those doe eyes. Her tiny skirt is so tight that all I can think about is ripping it off and taking her right here in my fucking living room.

"I am going to get ready for bed. Did you want to talk in the morning?" Her voice is low. Uncertainty laces her sweet melodic tone.

"No. We're doing this now." I step into the hallway, blocking her from progressing toward the bedroom. I reach out and grasp her wrist, pulling her to me. She stumbles into my hold so that we're inches apart, and this time, I'm not letting her go. Her smooth, creamy skin is flushed, her tongue darts out and wets those delicious plump lips.

I reach up and twist a lock of her hair around my finger as my gaze drinks her in. "Do you even realize how much I want you?"

"No, Liam, I don't. Because ever since I arrived, you've pushed me away. So, I don't know. Let me go. I'm tired." She places a small, delicate hand flat on my chest, which sends a shiver of desire rippling through me. I'm sure she can feel my heart thudding against her palm.

"You really want me to leave you alone?"

She's quiet for a long while and her eyes bore into mine. Chocolate to hazel. "Yes." The breathy word stops my heart. I don't want to. There's no way I could ever willingly let her go, and the honesty in her conviction rocks me. Never has a woman seized my attention the way she does, and I don't even fucking know her. Not the way I want to.

The only thing I do know is how she moans and whimpers when I drive into her. The way her body shudders when she lets go and her orgasm rocks her. And the feel of her soft, smooth skin under my fingers, lips, and tongue. But I want more.

I want to look into her soul, embed myself so deep in the marrow of her being, that she can never forget me. I want the rhythm of our hearts to beat in the same way I do when I find the rapid cadence on the drums.

For the first time, I want to know someone on a deeper level than just fucking. She's fighting me, I know I wanted her to, but I've changed my mind. Her face is void of emotion.

I step forward, closing the distance between us. I am still holding on to her wrist. My grip tightens as she takes a tentative step back. When she finds her back flush with the wall, her breathing hitches, and my heart thumps against my chest.

I lean in, my lips barely brushing her cheek. The shiver that runs over her body at my proximity doesn't go unnoticed. My voice is low, controlled, but there is something dark in my tone. "You're telling me that I should walk away? Just let you go? That if I pushed my hand between your thighs and ripped those panties off, you wouldn't be soaking wet for me?"

"Liam, please—"

"Please? Oh darling, you don't have to beg, but I love it when you do." The glare she pins me with is adorable, sexy, and I need to bend her over and ram into her tight body. I reach up with my free hand and run my thumb over her bottom lip. It's plump, pink, and wet. The ache to bite it, tug it, and suck it into my mouth has me groaning.

"That's not what I meant." Her sassy mouth is as bad as her sister's. And it turns me the fuck on. What I wouldn't do to fuck her right now.

"You sure? Because from where I'm standing, it sounds like you need it. You need me. Inside you, deep, and so fucking hard." I lift her chin with my index finger until her eyes lock on mine. There's something in there. Emotion. She does want this. I want this. *Why is she pushing me away? Because I pushed her away.*

"No. I don't need you." With that, she pushes against my chest again, and this time I release her. Then she turns and walks away. Watching her retreating form is agony. She's gotten under my skin. The need to be with her, to see her smile, to fuck her—it's overwhelming. No woman has brought me to my knees. *Why her?*

The door of the guest room shuts with a final click. Followed by silence. It surrounds me, threatening to choke me. I don't know what to do with this, the want I have for her. My phone buzzing pulls me from my thoughts. "What?"

"What the hell crawled up your ass?" Ryan asks on the other end of the line.

"Nothing." He's my best friend, so he'll know something is up before I've had a chance to say anything. He's quiet for a beat.

"Did you fuck her yet?" I stalk back into the living room, not wanting to get into this conversation where she can hear me.

"No, I haven't. So you can't give me shit about it. I've been behaving. I want her, so fucking bad. Her smile is killing me, man. I want to see it all the time. She's different, feisty, and so fucking sexy."

"And how blue are your balls?"

"Probably the same as yours," I bite back.

"Fuck you, man." Chuckling, I unlock the terrace door and step out into the warm night. I love the West Coast. The sea air is refreshing. I stand and watch the waves crash on the shore.

"You do know that Kierra isn't going to wait forever for you to get your shit together, right?" His heavy sigh tells me that he knows I'm right. The woman is a piece of dynamite, and I can tell she reciprocates his feelings.

"I know, but this call wasn't about me. It's about you and Em. What are you going to do?" The stars are out, and I feel like a swim. I have a private cove just off my patio, which allows me a secluded area of the beach that I want to take advantage of tonight. A cool dip in the ocean might calm me down.

"I don't know. I need a swim. See you tomorrow?"

"Yeah. Don't lose her and don't be a dick."

He's goading me as he always does and I don't stop my retort. "Fuck you."

"Yeah, you too." We hang up, and I drop my phone on the patio chair. Tugging my shirt off, I drop it on the seat and my jeans follow.

The need for a drink is rife. I have to stop the ache in my chest. That knowing feeling that I wouldn't be able to stop at one. This is why Callum is so worried.

Heading to the water dressed in my boxer briefs, my skin instantly cools. But the heat that flows through my veins for the feisty brunette doesn't waver.

EMMA

Standing on the terrace, I watch his muscles tense as the waves crash against his body. I overheard his conversation, which I'm guessing was with Ryan and not Callum. There is no way he would have been so honest about his feelings for me if he were talking to his brother.

His wet skin shines under the full moonlight, and I find myself licking my lips. He's handsome in a rugged, rough way. His broad shoulders and lean torso are sculpted and toned. His deep-tanned skin is like caramel, and I want to lick him.

Maybe, just maybe, I can convince him to give us a chance. Without thinking about it any longer, I strip down to my underwear and race toward the water. He's deeper in than I thought, and he doesn't notice me until I am right behind him. "Liam." My voice is soft, and the crashing waves seem to drown out the sound.

I know he's heard me, though, because his body tenses, and he spins around to find me wet and stripped down to my underwear. "Fuck." The word tumbles from his lips as his hungry gaze scorches my skin. He hasn't touched me, but I feel like his hands are on every inch of my skin, just from one look. "What are you doing, Peach?"

"I figured a midnight swim would be fun." I shrug nonchalantly. Reaching back, I unclasp my bra and toss it back onto the sand. When I face Liam, his gaze is locked on my now-pebbled nipples. My body is aching for him—for his lips and mouth to devour every inch of me.

A growl echoes through the night, and I know he's barely holding on to his restraint. "Em, babe, you need to not do this." His words cut, but I am not going to take no for an answer this time. I can see he wants me. *So, why is he pushing me away?*

Waves splash against me and I shiver. When I reach for him, the warmth of his skin ignites a fire deep in my core. I peek up at the flames dancing in his hazel eyes. His desire is clear as day, and as soon as I reach for him, it's like I manage to break through a glass case because everything around us shatters, and his mouth devours mine. His heated kiss sears my lips as I moan into his mouth. I feel rough, calloused hands travel down my back and grip my ass in a vise grip.

He lifts me against him and his thick, heavy cock presses against me. Instinctively, I wrap my legs around him, feeling the crown nudging my core. All that separates us is the thin material of his briefs and my panties. His tongue fights mine for control, and I let him claim it. Claim me.

When we finally break apart, I stare into his now dark brown eyes that remind me of rich, black coffee. "I want you. Stop fighting it." My words tumble in the darkness, like the waves that are crashing around us.

"Fuck it." The air that swirls around us is laden with hunger and desire, igniting a fire within me. Our bodies mold together, his hardness and my softness, perfectly in sync. His one hand snakes between us and when his fingers reach my core, he growls into my mouth. He shifts the material of my underwear to the side, and two thick fingers dip into my body, sending me reeling.

The slow pumping of his hand causes my body to lock, and I am a whimpering mess when he finally pulls both digits from my wet pussy.

His voice is a growl as he walks us out of the water. "You're so fucking beautiful when you come apart by my hand. I need to be inside you. Hold on to me, Peach." My arms wrap tightly around him as he leans down to retrieve my discarded bra. He continues into the house and sets me on the sofa. I'm still dripping wet, but he doesn't seem to mind. With a click he turns on the fireplace and it roars to life.

"Sit here, baby." He reaches a hand out to me and tugs me onto the soft white shag carpet in front of the fire. The heat warms the chill, and I watch Liam stalk over to the door, grab his phone, and shut the door.

"Liam..." I trail off when he walks over to a door in the hallway and pulls out two soft towels. When he joins me again, he wraps the towel around me and plants a soft kiss on my forehead.

Cupping my face in his large hands, he tilts my head back so I am looking directly into dark eyes. "I do want you, but I need time to tell my brother. He doesn't trust me with you. I don't trust me with you, and that's what matters. There's something you don't know about me and before you make a choice, I need to tell you."

I kneel and tug the towel tighter around me. The fire warms the large open area, but being this close to Liam while he's sitting in his briefs is very distracting. "Can you put clothes on?" I question with a giggle. But the naughty smirk that curls those sexy, full lips has me squirming.

"Why? Does my body distract you, Peach?" When I swat his shoulder, my towel drops and his gaze immediately falls to my bare breasts.

"Yes, the same way my body distracts you, Hayes." Thick arms wrap around me, pulling me against him. My laugh breaks any tension there was between us as his fingers find my hips and he tickles me relentlessly. My breathing is ragged, but I can't stop laughing. He rolls us over until I'm straddling his waist.

"You make everything fucking distracting, gorgeous."

I don't know what expression comes across my face at his words, but any remnants of the light laughter we were sharing just a moment ago come to a halt. "What about all those girls you have on tour with you?" As soon as the question falls from my mouth, I feel him tense below me.

"No. Just you." The way his eyes shimmer with the truth makes me smile. Does he really mean that? I want to believe that there's even the slightest chance that I can tame the bad boy drummer.

"Just me?" I lean in and place a soft kiss on his chest. The ink that adorns his skin is beautiful, and I can't help smiling at the intricate patterns. He's like a walking canvas.

"I know you don't believe me, and I'm going to do everything I can to prove it to you. Since I saw you in London, I couldn't take my eyes off you." That statement has me straightening. My body still bare to his gaze.

"Really? So you mean to tell me that since then—pretty much six months ago—you haven't slept with anyone else?" I stare at him incredulously. There's a naughty smirk playing on his lips, and I have a feeling I'm in for it now. Rough hands grip my hips, and he moves me back and forth slowly. My core rubbing against the steel in his briefs.

"Do you mean to tell me that since that night in London, you've been able to think about anyone else?" He raises my challenge with another, and I grin. Placing both hands on his ripped chest, I feel his heart thudding against my hand.

"I asked you first, drummer boy. Now, be honest." Biting my cheek to keep from giggling at his expression for my nickname for him, I watch the wheels turning in his head.

"Honestly?" he questions and I nod, I asked for it. "I slipped up once, a one-off blow job. Other than that there hasn't been anyone in my bed for six months. Since you, I've been a very good boy." The last few words come out as a low growl, which shudders through me. His voice is rough with desire, lighting the spark inside me. His confession doesn't hurt, it's refreshing and I can see it in his eyes, there's no denying what's between us.

"You? A good boy? I doubt that." I roll my eyes and he chuckles. The flirty playfulness doesn't stop when he suddenly rolls us over and I find myself beneath him, his body pinning me to the soft carpet.

When he leans in, my eyes flutter closed, and I wait for a kiss that doesn't come. Instead, I feel his hot breath on my ear. "Yes, I was a good boy. But now I want to be bad."

LIAM

"I thought you wanted to talk to me first?" Her question catches me off guard. Yes, there is a lot I need to tell her, to explain to her, but right now, all I can think of is driving my cock into her tight body and making her scream my fucking name.

"Talking can wait. I want your legs wrapped around my waist, your tight pussy squeezing my cock, and your nails digging into me as you arch your back while you're screaming my name."

"You've clearly thought about this, haven't you?" Her giggle is musical. Ignoring her question, I feather kisses along the nape of her neck, causing a trail of goosebumps to rise in response. I suck the soft skin into my mouth, my teeth graze the sensitive flesh, and she shudders under me. Lowering my mouth, I lave her hardened nipple, biting down just enough to have her mewling like a kitten. Her body is writhing below me—just where I want her. The sweet scent of her is intoxicating, and every fear I had flies out the window as my mouth latches on to her other nipple.

I suckle it as her fingers fist in my hair, holding me where she needs me. I peer up at her under hooded lids and see her lips part in soft moans and whimpers. "Liam." Her moaning my name is enough to have me coming in my briefs.

As I move down her body, dipping my tongue in her belly button has another sexy, soft whimper tumbling from her lips. My fingers tug on her panties, pulling them down smooth, creamy thighs. Her bare cunt is glistening with desire, and all I can think about is tasting her. "Open your legs, baby." She does, and I press a kiss on her inner thigh. Her hips rise up and I chuckle. "So naughty, aren't you? Does my Peach want me here?" When she moans again as I release a soft breath on her core, I have my answer.

"God, Liam, stop teasing me." Her big, brown eyes are wide as she watches me. Flattening my tongue, I lap at her pussy. The first taste is overwhelming, and I realize she's my addiction. No amount of time will be enough with her. The thought scares me because I haven't ever wanted more than one night. It's always been easy to walk away, but as I slide my tongue inside her, all that flies out the window. Her body pulses around my tongue and her fingers once again grip my hair, pulling, tugging, and the biting pain has me growling against her delectable pussy.

"Ride my face, baby. Take your pleasure." My words are muffled, but the way her hips move tells me she had no trouble hearing them. And ride she does. Her hips move back and forth as she fucks my mouth. Riding my tongue until suddenly she stiffens and screams out my name. *My fucking name.*

"Fuck, Liam…" Her words taper off, and I watch her body tremble with the aftershocks of her orgasm. She's so fucking beautiful. When her eyes meet mine, she grins and pushes up onto her elbows. "What?"

"You're incredibly beautiful when you come. Make me so fucking hard." I crawl over her, my arms on either side of her, and our lips crash together in a heated kiss.

"Fuck me, Liam," she whispers, and nothing has ever sounded sweeter. My hips buck and I tease her smooth lips with my cock. "Please."

Without another word, I slide into her. She's so wet from her earlier orgasm that my full nine inches slide into her with ease. Her tight heat pulses around my shaft, and it takes all my restraint not to come. I move slowly, sliding in and out, teasing her inch by inch as I slip back in. The torture isn't only for her, because my body is humming, aching to drive into her, fuck her, possess her. As the thought enters my mind, my body comes alive with the desire to make her forget any other man. To make her want me and only me. To have her body need mine.

Driving into her, I move faster. Her nails

dig into my back, just like I wanted, needed, ached for. "Look at me, Peach. Your eyes on me. I'm fucking you." Her big, chocolate eyes peer up under hooded lids, and her lips are parted in soft sighs as I thrust into her.

"You feel so good. Fucking me. Destroying me. Claiming me." Her words shatter my calm façade, causing my chest to tighten. There's emotion in her gaze— emotion I longed for—and now when I see it, I break. Completely shatter in this beautiful girl's arms.

The bad boy manwhore is falling, and nobody will be able to catch me but her. Our bodies move in a rhythm of our hearts thudding as one. "Come for me, Peach. All over my cock. I need to feel you." Her body convulses and she cries out again and again. My name echoes through the empty living room as she moans while her pussy pulses and tightens around me. The pure ecstasy on her face is my undoing. My balls tighten, and hot spurts of cum shoot deep inside her. Our bodies collide and tremble and we hold on to each other.

My addiction. My salvation. My sweet, exquisite Peach.

It's quiet with only the fire crackling in the background. Her soft breaths calm my heartbeat into a steady rhythm. I need to talk to her, but the fear that she'll walk away, that she won't be able to accept me for who I am, eats at me.

I know I have to come clean at some point. My past isn't the brightest, and someone as sweet and innocent as Emma Quinn may not understand it.

As much as I was pushing her away, I was pulling her toward me. Having her in my arms helps quell the desire for something that will only ruin my life. Again. "Why so serious?" I glance down at her in the dim light and smile. Her sweet voice is beautiful. A salve to my open wounds. The gaping holes that leave me bleeding on a daily basis. She needs to know about my past, about the things I've done.

"Just thinking." I trail a finger down her cheek until I reach her chin then continue the trail lower, between her breasts and then dipping into her navel. Her breath catches, sending desire flooding through me. When I reach her smooth pussy, her legs part slightly and a soft moan catches in the back of her throat. With one thick finger, I dip into her cunt. It's so warm, slick, and tight. With a slow stroke, I finger-fuck her, drawing out her nectar mixed with my release, circling her clit, making her hips buck and her fingers dig into my shoulder.

"About?"

"About you." I dip my finger in again and add another digit. Her body opens for me. Accepting me. Sliding in and out, I draw the pleasure from her core. From the sweet, innocent soul who I will surely tarnish with my blemishes. With the darkness that has plagued me for so long.

"Liam."

"Shh, Peach." My fingers move faster and faster, dipping deeper with every stroke until I crook my fingers and rub the spot that sends her crashing into delirium as she cries out my name again. The sound of her coming—screaming only my name—is a boost to my caged heart. I want to be worthy of her. To be someone she can one day call her husband.

Jesus, Hayes, you're going soft. Marriage? "You're so fucking perfect." My words still her, and when she glances at me, the smile that splits her face is radiant. It lights up the room, but more than that, it lights the darkness in my heart.

"Liam, why do you look so sad when your fingers are inside me?" Her question drags me from the abyss, and I chuckle as I slowly move my hand. Her body trembles beneath me. Without thinking, I lick each finger while my gaze is locked on hers. She watches intently as I clean my fingers of her sweet arousal.

"You taste like sunshine on a rainy day." Her giggle is light, and it seems her three orgasms have her spent. Those incredible lashes flutter closed and her breathing soon evens. She's so relaxed. Her face is serene, and it makes my heart ache.

Xxx

My eyes crack open and I feel a warm

body molded to mine. Her scent is sweet and alluring and as much I'd like to take her again, I know she needs to rest. So much has happened over the past twenty-four hours and there's still the topic of my past I need to tell her about.

I slip out from under her arm and pad over to the kitchen. I grab a glass and fill it with chilled water from the fridge. I glance behind me to the most beautiful woman I've ever been lucky enough to have in my bed sprawled on my white carpet. Her smooth skin glows with the soft light from the fire. She's perfect, and I can't help my cock throbbing to be inside her again.

Staring out of the window, I'm lost in thought when her soft voice calls out to me. "Is something wrong?" I turn to find her peering at me.

"I'm wondering how to make this work, Emma. I'm not good with relationships. Hell, I'm not good with morning afters." Raking my hand through my hair, I find myself at a loss for words.

"What? You're just going to fuck me and

discard me like your other bimbos?" She's up on her feet in seconds, storming toward me. Thank fuck she's got the towel wrapped around her because her nakedness won't help my concentration.

"Baby, I am not discarding you. I'm navigating unknown territory for me here." When I reach out for her, she flinches, which angers me. I don't want her anger. For the first time in my life, I realize I want a woman's love instead. But not just any woman—the one standing in front of me, looking at me like I just ripped her heart out.

Right here, at this moment, I have to decide. I need to choose between being the man I was or being the man I know I can be. The one who can make her smile.

EMMA

"Liam, I am not a little girl anymore. If you don't want me, be honest and tell me. Right here, right now." His gaze does a slow ascent up my body, leaving heat in its trail. A shiver runs over me, and suddenly, I'm in his arms. His mouth is poised an inch away from mine. Then he whispers over my lips.

"I want you more than you can even imagine, Peach. First, we should talk and I'll explain why my brother is so against us being together." My heart stutters at his honesty. The words that linger in my mind tell me he wants me. They bathe me in warmth and belief that maybe I can tame this beast.

"So then explain, because I am not going anywhere. You can't scare me off." My voice is louder than I intended and those hazel eyes bore into me.

"Let's get dressed. I can't concentrate with you in a fucking towel." Rolling my eyes, I spin on my heel and before I can get away from him, he slaps my ass. The tiny yelp that escapes my lips has him groaning, and I love the power it gives me to know that I have such a hold on him. That I can turn him on with a simple sound.

In the bedroom, I pull on my sweats and a floppy tee. This shouldn't be too distracting for him. As I pad back to the living room, he's sitting on the sofa. The fire is still blazing, and I take in the reflection of the flames that dance across his tanned torso. His unruly hair is sticking up in all directions, and I have the urge to run my fingers through it again.

He glances up, but instead of the playfulness that's always in his gaze, there's pain running through his caramel eyes, which lurches my heart. This must be bad.

"Sit with me." I take his outstretched hand and slide onto the sofa next to him. The heat of his body envelops me, and the rich scent of his spicy cologne calms me somewhat. That is until he looks at me. And the agony I see in his gaze makes me feel like climbing into his lap and holding him close.

"Liam, you don't have to do this if you don't want to."

"I do. If you're going to be with me, then you need to know about my past." He inhales a deep breath before he starts. "When I was a kid, I looked up to my father. He was my hero." He chuckles sadly but continues. "One day, after I had turned sixteen, I got home from school—which I hated, by the way—and found him on the sofa in his briefs and nothing else. He looked so broken. When I went up to him, I noticed he was drunk. He didn't even hear me walk into the house."

He stops and turns to the fire, and the flames dance across his face. The mood is somber, and my heart is racing in my chest. "I wasn't there to stop him. My father was an alcoholic. He'd lost his job and he went into a depression that he stayed in until…" Liam's body shudders with the memory that is so clearly killing him to remember. Without thinking, I climb into his lap and straddle him. Cupping his face in my hands, I feel his stubble, rough against my palms.

"Hey, you don't have to tell me this now."

"Emma, I found him..." He takes another deep inhale, and my body is now shaking with trepidation. "...He was hanging in our bathroom three months later." Caramel eyes that usually held such affection for me are now glazed over, and the ache in my chest for this broken man cracks my heart wide open. A loud gasp is all I manage because my mind can't fathom how a sixteen-year-old boy wouldn't be severely scarred after seeing something like that.

"Liam, I am so sorry. I mean, there isn't anything I can say that will make it right or okay..." My voice trails off when he looks at me.

"There's more." He offers a rueful smile. "I am, was, well... Fuck. I was an addict for a long time. I was in and out of rehab for years. My brother dragged my ass back and forth. I would be sitting behind bars, or worse, lying dead somewhere if it weren't for him. I fucked women because they were objects. I treated them like shit because most of the time I didn't know what I was doing. The next morning, I wouldn't remember anything." His voice is a low growl. "I'm still battling a lot of that. Every day is an uphill battle. The ache to pick up a bottle, the need to drink runs in my veins. Jesus, I can't even stay clean for very long."

Lifting me, he places me on the sofa and pushes up, stalking to the fireplace. With one hand gripping the brick mantel, I watch the muscles in his back tense. His knuckles are white with the tight grasp he has on the brick, and I am certain it's going to crumble.

It's quiet, but I can hear his deep breaths. The tears I have been holding on to spill as I blink. "Liam, please don't push me away. Everybody has skeletons in their closet. Life isn't easy. It's difficult, shit, but you're stronger than that." He turns slowly and methodically, his gaze is heated and sad at the same time, making my head spin.

"I wish I could give you what you want and what you need, but I shouldn't be in a relationship. I'm too vulnerable and I become dependent. If it didn't work out, I'd break. My willpower is non-existent."

"So, you're just walking away?" My question hovers between us, and he shrugs, which makes me angry. "Look, I can't begin to understand what you went through. But to be honest with you, I think you're pushing me away out of fear. You're scared to let someone love you because you don't love yourself."

"You don't understand." The frustration in his tone is clear, and he's right, I don't understand. "I can't do this. If I fall off the wagon and do anything, like hurt you..."

"You won't. Liam don't—"

"It's what I do, Emma!" His voice booms through the living room. "I will not be able to live with myself if I did." With that, he storms away, leaving me gaping at his outburst. All I hear is the slamming of his bedroom door as he shuts himself away again.

He is so infuriating. He doesn't have

to treat me like I'm fragile. The truth hurts more with him shutting me out. Padding to my room, I shut the door with a soft click and grab my phone. I know it's late, but my sister will have to listen to me whine. As soon as I hear her voice, tears well in my eyes.

"Em, are you okay?"

"Liam, he's... I mean..." A frown furrows my brows.

"I know. Callum's on the phone with him. God, can either one of you ever behave yourselves?" Her incredulous tone would have me giggling if I wasn't so heartbroken. I like Liam, a lot. More than I want to admit. But the fact that he's gone to his brother for advice makes me feel better about our fight. Perhaps he'll see reason.

"Well, he's being an ass."

"And how do you figure that, little sister?"

She saw us together in London. She can't tell me that she doesn't remember the way he treated me, like I was precious to him. Even Callum saw it because he told me he'd never seen his brother smile so much. "Tay, don't tell me you haven't noticed it. We work. Me and him. In our fucked-up-ness, we work." She's quiet and I know she's contemplating my words.

"I don't want you to get hurt. You do realize you can't change him, right? You need to accept him as is and just be there. What if things get rough? Are you going to run like you always do?" Her words sink into my heart. She's right. Every time I have ever had something difficult to deal with, I've fled. When my parents told me they were moving to London, I jumped at the chance to go. Running from the boy who wanted me to move in with him, when I realized he was in love with me and I couldn't handle the pressure of a long-term relationship. Every time life threw me a curveball, I dodged it and made my escape. *Can I handle Liam at his worst?* If it came to that, I think I could. Although it's not enough to *think*. I need to be sure.

LIAM

"I told you to keep your dick in your pants, but you never listen, do you?" Callum's voice is low. He's probably worried Tayla will overhear.

"I told her. She knows about everything." He knows how difficult it is for me to talk about shit. About my past.

"Everything?" His question grates me.

"Yes, everything."

His heavy sigh comes through the line. "Are you sure you're not going to fuck this up? Because you know this isn't a game to her. If you hurt her…"

"I know. Don't lecture me." I plead. I want him to trust me.

His response is brutal, but honest. "I don't have a choice, brother." Crashing onto my bed, I shut my eyes. All I see are those pretty brown ones. That long, flowing brown hair. Those amazing tits. Groaning, I push up off the bed. "She could be your salvation, but you need to decide if you're willing to take the chance and follow through. Do you understand?"

"Yeah." My body's in pain. The tour took a toll on me and the upcoming local shows will be our last—we all know it. Cal doesn't want to admit it, but I can't do this anymore. The knock on my door drags me from my worried thoughts. "Give me a second," I call out. "I got to go, I'll see you in a few days." Once I've hung up, I push off the bed.

As soon as I open the bedroom door, those big doe eyes peer up at me. "Hey." Her voice is wary, but fuck, she's so beautiful.

"Hey." A soft pink dusts her cheeks and her plump rose-colored lips quirk into a smile. "You're an ass, Liam Hayes."

Nodding, I can't help but smirk. "Yeah, I know, darling. I have been for a long time and I lost it back there. The pressure of not going down a dark road again is a lot to take on for me."

"I thought you just wanted to be single so you could fuck anything with two legs." That smart mouth. I chuckle at her, but the glare she pins me with has the sound hanging in the space between us. Reaching up, I stroke her cheek with the back of my fingers. Her skin is like silk under my touch.

"Peach, if I just wanted to fuck anything with two legs, I wouldn't be standing here now, making my choice."

She's perfect and I've never felt like a man worthy of much, but as I look at her, and I mean really take her in, I can see the happiness beaming from her.

"So you're not going to man-whore yourself anymore?"

"No, baby. If you want this, then I do too." I pull her closer. The stress that permeates my thoughts is gone. "I want to take you on a date tomorrow," I mumble in her hair.

"I would like that." She peers up at me smiling.

I've decided to take her to dinner and show her the side of me that women have never seen. As we pull up to the small diner, my fingers find her lower back as I lead her beside me. This is outside of my comfort zone, being on a date.

Once we're seated, I ask the waitress for a bottle of sparkling water, and we peruse our menus. Although, there's something else that has my attention and she's sitting across from me. "Are you going to stare at me all night, Mr. Hayes?" Emma's teasing will get her a spanking later, but I can't stop myself from smiling.

"I am. There's a beautiful woman in my company, and I can't take my eyes off her." She drops her chin, and I can see the blush on her cheeks. I may not be the romantic type, but with her, I'm willing to try.

"I like you, Liam. I know this isn't going to be easy, but I want to be here." The sincerity in her tone tugs at my heart, and my emotions are all over the place.

"I like you, baby." I reach for her hand and

she slips hers into mine. When our skin touches, it's as if there's a fire scorching me. Electricity flows between us, and as scared as I was, and still am, I know this woman will be there for me through anything.

With all the shit I've been through, I want nothing more than to show her I can be what she needs. In the bedroom and out of it. The waitress comes back with our water, a Coke for myself, and Emma's fruit juice. Seeing her order something non-alcoholic is evidence enough that this woman cares. That she'll own my heart. Somewhere deep down, I know she owns it already.

I can't believe it's Friday already. Spending this past week with Emma has given me new confidence to work at a relationship with her. Spending time with her as a couple has been eye-opening. The radio blares as we make our way to Napa. Her parents opted to stay in LA today and head up for the wedding tomorrow morning. Yesterday was probably my favorite day.

I made her a special dinner and gave her the honesty I'm slowly learning to come to terms with.

"When did you become so romantic, drummer boy?" Her naughty gaze is pinned on me, watching my every move. I've lit candles all around the living room. The dinner I cooked, from scratch, is plated and waiting for us to devour it. But I take my time, walking her to the table, pulling out the chair, and waiting on her, bringing her a glass of wine. I know she'd rather not drink, but I am strong enough to get through a dinner. I know I can.

"Since I met this girl, you see, she's seemingly turned my world upside down," I say as I slip into the seat opposite her. Picking up my sparkling water, I wait for her to do the same with her wine glass. "You're an incredible force of nature. Like a tornado crashing into my life, knocking me on my ass, you've taught me to feel more in a few days than I have in months, years even. I want us to work, Emma." When I finish my speech, I see the tears shimmering in her eyes. Without another word, she nods.

"Me, too." Those two words are my anchor, holding me steady in the uncertainty that my life has become..

The drive to Napa was long, but having my girl beside me was perfect. As I pull up to the vineyard, I park the SUV and jump out, rounding the car to help Emma. As I'm pulling the luggage out of the trunk, my brother and Tayla join us. The sisters hug each other, and I can tell they've missed one another.

"Brother, are you two okay?" I glance at Callum and nod with a big smile. He returns it, and the tension in him fades.

"Liam, you big oaf." Tayla grabs me in a tight hug, and I lift her, spinning her around. Her squeal is loud and I chuckle. She's a slight, petite little thing, both sisters are. As we head inside, I turn to my sister-in-law.

"Your folks will drive up alone. They asked if they could have a day in LA, so they'll arrive tomorrow." She nods.

"Mom called and told me. Thanks for waiting for them."

"It's no problem, let's get checked in, baby." I turn to my girl, and everyone stares at me. "What?" Callum chuckles and slaps me on the back.

"Just never thought I'd see the day, brother." His words ring true because I never thought I'd see the day, either. It's been a long time coming, but I know that I need to change. I want to change.

As soon as Emma and I are checked in, we make our way to the room. It's spacious and the bed is huge—perfect for long nights of making love. "This is amazing." She twirls around and the shorts she's wearing have my eyes glued to her pert little ass, making my mouth water. I think she should tattoo "Peach" on it. I'd bite it every day.

EMMA

"Kierra, have you and Ryan done the nasty? I mean the way you two look at each other, it's as if you're about to rip each other to shreds." The three of us are sitting at a small, round table in the cellar of the winery, drinking the most incredible Merlot I've ever had.

"No, we have not done anything." Her tone is incredulous, but I can't help giggling. "We're not… I can't be with him, not yet." We all nod and gulp down more alcohol, which seems to be warming me up.

"You two should get it over with, just take the plunge. He wants you and you want him, it's obvious." My sister's voice is soft as I pull my beeping phone from my purse and Liam's name blinks at me.

*Get up, walk up the stairs, turn right. *

Slipping my phone back into my purse, I turn to Tayla. "Watch my purse, I need to find the restroom." The girls nod as I head toward the staircase.

I reach the top of the stairs and turn right, as instructed. It's quiet, and I'm sure we came in through the other hallway. Suddenly, a hand tugs me into a room and I am plunged into darkness. "My sweet, sexy Peach. I need you." Liam's deep baritone is hoarse. I recognize the lust in his tone.

"What are you doing here? Aren't you boys supposed to be having a bachelor party?" I hiss into the dark. He's got me pinned between his hard body and the wall. The heat of his breath fans over my cheek, and a whimper slips from my lips when I feel his tongue trace the shell of my ear.

"This"—his hand drops between my legs—"is what I want to do. This sweet pussy needs attention, and I'm aching to fuck you deep and hard." Suddenly, he spins me around and pulls me with him. The office we're in overlooks the restaurant and the tasting room.

There are people milling around the high tables, and the dining room is packed. "What are you doing?" The window allows us to see them, but can they see us?

"I told you, I'm going to fuck you. Hands on the window." I obey his command and bend at the waist. He lifts my short red skirt over my hips. When he takes in the thong I'm wearing, I hear another deep growl.

"You like?" I wiggle my ass toward him, and a loud slap rains down on my ass cheek, eliciting a yelp from me.

"Don't fucking tease me, baby." He presses against me, and I feel his thick erection against me. His rough hands grip my ass and he growls. "Mine."

I hear shuffling, then without warning I'm filled, stretched, taking him deep inside my body. People shuffle around below us as he fucks me, sending waves of pleasure through my body. My blood heats with desire, and my orgasm tightens low in my stomach. That familiar pleasure, the ache easing with every slow thrust of his thick, hard cock. My toes curl as desire coils like a snake, tightening, tugging, waiting to strike. It's hot, dirty, and I love being fucked while people unknowingly wander around downstairs.

"Liam... please?" The words strangle in my throat as his fingers find my clit, rubbing slow circles around it, teasing me. Keeping me on the precipice of oblivion. The ache burns from my core, deep within my very being.

"You're so fucking perfect, my gorgeous girl." His words are strained with his own pleasure, his release not far off. "I want you with me, baby. I want that pretty pussy to squeeze me, to soak me in your sweet fucking cum that I'm going to draw from your very fucking soul." His words ignite a primal ache in my gut, and I fly over the edge as his fingers pinch my sensitive bud.

Liam's body locks, and his ejection thickens inside me, filling me more than I ever thought was possible. His hot seed shooting inside me. Owning me. Making me his.

We stand silently, catching our breath. He softens inside me, and when he slips out, I can't help wincing at the emptiness I feel without him.

"Let me clean you up baby."

"That was naughty, Liam." I giggle, watching him on his knees in front of me, cleaning me with the tissue he pulled from his jeans pocket. I smooth my skirt down and glance at my favorite panties, now a ripped scrap of material on the floor.

"I'll take care of this." He grabs them and shoves them in his jeans.

"And you expect me to walk around the rest of the night without underwear?" I stare at him in the dimly lit room.

"Yes, and when you get to the hotel room later, I'm going to make you come again on my tongue, my fingers, and then my cock." A cheeky wink, and then he laces his fingers through mine.

"I really need the restroom," I whisper as we head toward the staircase.

"Okay, darling. I'll be at the table." I nod

and plant a soft kiss on his scruffy cheek. His stubble is a day old and feels incredible against my heated skin.

He heads downstairs and I turn to find the restrooms. They were down here somewhere. I love how Liam takes charge with me, makes me feel cared for, cherished, and wanted. I would almost say loved.

It's only been a few days that we've been dating. I don't want to get ahead of myself, but I know I'm falling for him. It's something I never wanted to do. Fall in love. But with Liam, it comes naturally. That need to be with him all the time. Every second of the day.

I push open the door of the ladies' and find it empty. A cold breeze has goosebumps rise on my skin. I'm going to kill him for making me walk around without panties. Heading into one of the stalls, I lock the door. I can hear the soft music and voices from downstairs filter up.

At the sink, I glance in the mirror and gasp at my messy hair and rake my fingers through it. The warmth of the wine and the buzz of the orgasm still has my body thrumming.

As I turn to leave, the door clicks and I come face-to-face with familiar eyes. My heart kicks in my chest, and my body is no longer thrumming with pleasure, but shivering with fear. Cold, gray eyes bore into me—an evil glint visible in them—and I step back instinctively. "This is the ladies' room."

"Oh, I know that, love." A thick English/American accent has recognition hitting me. It's him. Even in the dim light, I can recognize that it's the man who stalked me in London.

"What are you—"

"I suppose your sister didn't tell you about me?" His accent flips, and the deep rumble of a West Coast accent is thick with sarcasm.

"My sister?" I stare at him in confusion with my heart clawing its way up my chest. "What does my sister have to do with this?"

A dark smirk curls his lips, and the evil glint I saw earlier flashes in a more sinister way. The terror that suddenly grips my throat makes it hard to breathe, hard to swallow. I need to get to Liam, to Tayla. "Your boyfriend can't save you now, *Peach.*" He drawls the nickname in a menacing tone, and the awareness that turns my stomach has tears springing to my eyes.

My eyes dart to the door, wishing for someone to walk in. Or knock, or just... anything. I shouldn't have walked in here alone. Where is everyone? Why isn't anyone opening the door?

As if he's read my mind, the words fall from his cracked lips. "You're not going anywhere until I get what I came for. What I promised your sister I would take all those years ago."

"What the fuck are you talking about?" Fear paralyzes me. Something must have happened to Tay, but for the life of me, I can't understand why she didn't tell me.

"Oh darling, I want you, and you're going to obey and come with me. Or your sister will pay for it with her life." The threat has bile rising in my gut. His chilling words snap me from my fear and send me into a trembling anger. I make for the door, trying to shove past him, but before I have time to react or scream he reaches out, grabbing a fistful of hair and yanking my head back.

He leans in and a gasp escapes my throat, echoing in the restroom. He presses a cloth to my mouth. My arms flail, but he's too strong and there's no way I can unhook myself from him.

His nose trails lightly up my neck and to my ear.

"Now I can see why he calls you, Peach. I can't wait to take a bite."

My mind whirls with thoughts of never seeing my family again. As my eyes flutter closed from the intoxicating scent on the cloth, a moment of regret plagues my mind. I regret not having told Liam that I love him while I had the chance.

LIAM

"Why isn't she back yet?" I question to no one in particular. It's been ten minutes since I left her in the hallway. I should have walked with her to the restroom, but I thought she'd be okay.

"I'll go and check." Tayla's voice is strained. I rise from my chair to accompany her, but she shakes her head. "Ki can come with me." Callum's face, etched with worry, puts me on edge.

"I'm going, I don't give a shit if it's the ladies' room." I push up and stalk up the stairs with the girls. I'm first to get to the door, shoving it open and stepping inside. It's chilly, but I make my way into every stall, opening the doors to make sure they're empty.

"Maybe she wasn't feeling well," Kierra suggests behind me, and I turn to stare at her.

"She was fine, I swear. There wasn't a thing wrong with her." My brows crinkle as I regard her. The lump in my throat is thick with fear and makes it difficult to swallow. We head back down and find Callum and Ryan waiting at the table. "It's fucking empty. Completely deserted."

"It's going to be okay," my brother mumbles, but I know it's a lie. Grabbing my phone, I hit Call on her number, but her purse vibrates on the table.

Dragging my eyes up, I see Tay and Kierra staring at the black leather bag. *Where the fuck is she?*

"One of the staff checked the men's room, as well, and there's no sign of her." Tayla's words sink in and pain hits my chest.

It's been four hours and I've been biting my fucking nails trying to figure out what to do. We've called the police, but they can't do much since it's not been twenty-four hours yet. "This is fucking ridiculous. I can't sit here and wonder what happened. I'm going to go and drive around the area." Pushing up from the sofa in our suite, I feel Tayla's soft hand on mine. Big, brown eyes peer up at me, the same eyes as my beautiful girl. They're shimmering with unshed tears.

"Please, find her," she pleads, and all I can do is nod because any words are lodged in my throat, threatening to choke me.

"I'm going with you, brother." Callum rises from his seat, pulling Tay into a hug.

Turning to Ryan, I lean down and whisper, "Stay with the girls."

Without another look, I turn to the door, keys in hand with fear twisting my gut, my brother hot on my heels. My restraint—the same restraint that keeps me from drinking, from falling into the dark hole that numbs me—is getting more difficult to hold on to.

"Liam." I turn to face the blue eyes of my brother. He knows me better than anyone, and he's worried. I can see it. Whenever I'm stressed out or in pain, the first thing I do is hit the bottle, the painkillers, anything to take the edge off.

When I have Emma, she's my drug. She's my addiction. It's one addiction I never want to walk away from. Going cold turkey and losing her will detonate everything I hold close. My heart, my mind, my very fucking soul.

"Don't Cal, no lectures needed. Let's just find her." Slipping into the driver's seat, I turn the key and the engine roars to life. "I need to find her."

I don't know if I'm telling him this or if I'm trying to convince myself. But there's nothing that's going to stand in my way. I need my fix, and she's somewhere out there.

"We will, I promise." Dragging my glare over to him, I find concern in his eyes. That's something about my brother—you can always tell how he feels by the look in those baby blues. It's like looking right into his soul.

"Don't make promises you aren't sure you can keep."

"I didn't mean it like that, Liam. I don't know what happened, but we'll find her." His response is quiet, almost a whisper.

If I find out that someone has taken her, I will use my bare hands to hurt the fucker. "Callum, I can't live without her." As we weave through the wine farm, the roads are dark and windy. I'm sure there are no houses or buildings out this way, but I'm not about to leave a single square inch of land untouched.

My heart constricts in my chest, suffocating me. I pull up onto a grassy hill, staring out the window. I can just make out the trees and vines. The sky is dark, ominous, as the branches stretch across each other.

"Liam, I know you're strong. You can make it through this. Do you love her? I mean, really love her?" His voice is tight with emotion. The roughness of his tone tells me that he's worried. My brother is empathetic, he picks up on emotions, and right now, I know he can feel the war waging inside me.

Right now, I am angry and scared.

"I fucking love her, Callum. She's my

strength. My lifeline." We stare at each other in the dark. The emotions flit over his face, in his eyes, and he knows how I feel. It's the way he feels about his soon-to-be wife.

Passion. Devotion. Love.

Yes, Liam Hayes is in love. Falling into the abyss of emotion. "I know. I can see it when you talk about her, when you look at her. Brother, there is nothing I wouldn't do to help you get her back. Just stay strong. Please?" His hand squeezes my shoulder in solidarity. He is always there for me, and if my mom knew what was going on, she'd be urging me to stay strong and push past my need to consume alcohol till I pass out.

There is only one thing in this world that can save me. Emma Quinn. We head back towards the other edge of the property, but it's so dark out. She must be close by.

"I will be fine. For her. For you. For mom."

"You also need to stay strong for you, Liam. You need to be the man she needs. Whatever the fuck happened, she is going to need you more than you can imagine. After what happened to Tay…" His words trail off, and I glance at him. "Fuck."

"What?" I question, staring at him.

Without answering me, he pulls out his phone and dials. After a couple of rings, Tay's voice comes through the speaker.

"Cal?"

"Your father's ex-business partner. Where was he being held?" She's silent, and we both glance at the phone. I pull into the parking spot outside the bed and breakfast. "Tay, baby?"

"He was arrested and held in San Francisco. Why?"

"I have a suspicion. We're outside. I'll talk to you when I get inside." He hangs up and makes another call, this time to our private investigator. "I need you to find information for me." He rattles off the name and last known whereabouts of a man I have never heard of.

As we make our way inside, I pin him with a questioning glare. "What's going on, Cal?"

"The man who hurt Tay, I have a feeling

it's him."

I stop dead in the middle of the reception area. "What?"

"He told her that he was going after her sister. This was a few years ago, but someone with a vendetta doesn't easily give up."

My body goes cold, and a pain that I am sure is about to rip me to pieces squeezes my heart. If he is the one who took Em, I will fuck him up so bad he'll never fucking walk again. Let alone breathe. I just want my girl.

As we walk into the living area, Tayla bounds into Callum's arms, tears running down her face. "Cal, she's gone. He's got her." Her voice is shrill, and the cold grip of fear rips me apart.

"What the fuck are you talking about, Tayla?" My voice is harsh, but I don't care. This is the woman I love. She hands me her phone, and the photo filling the screen has me wanting to hurl it at the wall.

Anger sweeps through every fiber of my being. "Liam, give me the phone." My brother pulls it from my grip, and I watch his face drain of color.

"We need to get her back. My fucking girl." The words come out as a low growl, and everybody stops to stare at me. Spinning on my heel, my fist connects with the wall and blood stains the cream-colored paint.

EMMA

Everything hurts, and as I try to move, a pain shoots down my leg. When I grab my thigh, I feel a sticky substance. I crack my eyes and take in my surroundings. It's dark and musty, but the wood paneling tells me that I am still at the vineyard. Shivers wrack my body.

There's a pounding in my head, and breathing is difficult. Reaching out, I push up and cry out in pain as it sears through me. My arm gives way, and I collapse onto the hard, cold floor.

"The pretty little peach is awake." A menacing voice reaches through the darkness, and I glace up to find the man with the gray eyes. "You better eat. It will soon be time, and I don't want you dying before I've had my chance for revenge." With that, he closes the door and leaves me in the dark room with a plate of food and a glass of water. I don't know where I am and my mind is foggy. Disorientated, like I've been drugged.

My heart aches. Liam must be looking for me. My sister, Callum, Ryan and Kierra, they must all be worried sick. Pushing myself up, I sit on the mattress. My legs are shaky, but I manage to stand. I walk over to the door, feeling my way against the wall and find the light switch. The dim bulb comes to life, and I take in my surroundings.

It's a small room with a single bed. The floor is dark, but the walls are gray with paintings hanging haphazardly along them. Picking up the plate and glass, I pad over to the bed and sit down slowly. My legs are freezing cold since I'm only wearing a skirt. Picking up the sandwich, I take a bite into it and groan. I'm starving and it's good.

Before long, both the glass of milk and the bread are finished. There are small windows higher up, and I can see the soft light of dawn spilling into the room. I don't know how long I've been here, or how long I've been sleeping, but my head feels groggy. My body aches everywhere, but it's my heart that's in tatters.

What could he want with me? How does he know Tay? All I want is Liam's strong arms around me, holding me and keeping me safe. I want to give him something to live for, maybe even a family.

I know he's falling for me as I have fallen for him. I should have told him, there were so many moments that I waited. Now, time isn't on my side, and I'm not sure what's going to happen. *Will I ever get that chance? To tell him how I feel?* My mind flits back to the last few days, the memories making my heart ache.

"Liam, let's go!" I call out to him. We've decided to spend the day on the beach, enjoying each other's company. It's been two days since he told me about his past. I can see he has been trying to be a boyfriend. It's difficult since he's recognized most times we're out, but for the most

part, he'll grab my hand and tell reporters I'm his girlfriend.

"Come here, Peach, if I catch you, I will spank your ass." Giggling, I run up the sandy embankment and glance back. As I reach the top, I see him not far behind. The waves crash on the shore and the hot sun heats my skin, nowhere near what Liam's gaze does. I turn to watch him run up the hill, my hands on my hips.

"You're slow, old man." I tease. He's eleven years older than me, but with a body like that, you'd think he was much younger. When he reaches me, he lifts me up, spinning me around, and my arms twine around his neck. When we come to a stop, I peer at him through my sunglasses.

"Old man? Would you like to be put across my knee? It seems my girl needs to remember to respect her elders." His raspy tone tightens the coil in my stomach and has my clit throbbing. I lean in and whisper in his ear.

"Why don't you teach me to behave?" His growl is evidence that my words had their desired effect.

"I think it's time for lunch." Our gazes lock

and I frown. We haven't brought any food up here, and it's a trek back down to the blanket we had set up. "I'm going to eat that sweet pussy right here." He slides me down his body, and I feel his erection pressing into me.

"Liam, you can't..."

"Peach, I can do anything I want." With a cheeky wink, he lays me down under the hot sun and continues to make me cry out his name.

Sadness scorches my heart, leaving it cold and barren without him. "I love you..." My voice rings in the room. Suddenly, the door opens and the man's figure darkens the doorway. He's tall with broad shoulders that just about fit through the small space. His face is rounded and he looks to be in his late forties, unshaven, and it looks as if he's not slept in days. His cold eyes glare at me, sending a shiver of fear racketing through me.

"Awww, isn't that cute. He loves you, too."

"What do you want with me? I don't even know who you are."

"You're my ticket to a new life, Emma Quinn. Don't you recognize me?" He steps closer, but I can't for the life of me place him. My mind flits through everyone I have met in recent years, but he just doesn't look familiar.

"No, I don't." He scowls, staring at me with anger.

"When your father had those big corporations investing their insurance premiums with us, I came up with the perfect plan. Add an extra percent on a premium here and there, nobody will know the difference. Those rich fuckers will pay anything to keep their assets safe. I had almost gotten enough to make sure I was taken care of. That's when your father noticed the numbers didn't add up." Shaking my head, I can't believe this vile man did that. I never knew the background to what happened, but the shock that he blames my father sends waves of anger through me. "He took everything from me. He could have had it all. Instead, he grew a conscience and fucked up my whole plan." My face must have shown the shock I felt, because when those steely eyes landed on me again, he smirked. "Now you remember me, don't you, little Emmy?"

His nickname has my stomach lurching in disgust. The man in front of me looks nothing like I remember. When I was still in school, he used to come by our house.

When we hit high school, I don't remember seeing him much, and not long after, my father told us we'd be moving. There was so much going on that I didn't think about why or how. All I knew was that my father had gotten a new job because he'd learned that his business partner was stealing money.

"But, you were gone. They arrested you." My voice sounds small, and I am certain he can smell the fear dripping from me.

"And then I came back, found your sister, and made sure that she'll always remember me. Did you know she was a whore?" His lips curve into a sinister smirk.

"What? No, my sister—"

"She tried to protect you by giving her body up to ensure the safety of her sister.

But you know what..." he takes a small step toward me, and I take one back. "You can't run and this time, I will get to taste the little Emmy." Swiftly, his hand grabs my hair, tugging it back until my eyes are locked on his.

Pinning me against the wall between his body and the cold cement, his hot, stale breath in my ear as he hisses the words, "I want to taste that sweetness that your boyfriend can't get enough of, that he had to fuck you in a dark office. Did you like that? Did you like him fucking you like a little slut?" My eyes sting with tears as he pulls my hair harder, burning pain shooting through my head.

"Please, don't do this. We can pay you. Is it money you want?" The tears roll down my face as soon as I blink, and his lips brush against my cheek. Fear runs through my veins, sending cold shivers through me.

"Just like your sister, a little whore. I don't need your money. You have something else I want, though." His hand trails up my leg, gripping my thigh so hard, causing me to cry out in pain. His body pushes against me, and I can feel his erection.

"Just let me go, please?" My begging falls on deaf ears as he continues to rub himself against me. Faster and faster. Disgust has bile rising to my throat and my eyes slam shut. A buzzing rings through the room, and suddenly he lets go. Stepping back, I watch him pull a phone from his pocket.

Before he answers, he glares at me. "I will be back." And with that, I'm left alone again in the room. Lying on the bed, I curl into myself and let the tears flow. He didn't do anything, but I feel dirty. Filthy. Disgusting. Liam would never want me now. Not tainted the way I am.

When the door opens moments later, he walks in holding a dress bag. "You're wearing this." Chucking it on the bed, I glance down and then back at him.

"What? I mean, where do I change?" Giving in isn't what I want to do, but I'm out of options. I can't fight him, he's twice my size, and not having eaten very much, I am weak.

"Right here, Peach. I like pretty little girls, and I would love to see what's under that whore skirt." His cold eyes trace their way up my bare legs, and an icy shiver wracks through me. "I said fucking drop the skirt." His tone is low and dangerous, and it's only then I see a silver glint. A knife.

The tears prick my eyes as I push up from the bed and unzip my skirt. The realization that Liam has my panties in his pocket sends a fresh wave of nausea through me. As the skirt pools at my feet, I tug the hem of my top down, hoping to cover myself to his filthy gaze.

"So pretty." Stalking towards me, he grazes his hand over my cheek, down my arm, until he reaches my ass. Squeezing it tight, eliciting a painful yelp from me. His thick fingers trail their way over my hips, and he spins me around, pushing against my back, forcing me to bend at the waist.

I feel the cool point of the blade as it slices through my top. My bra follows. My body is trembling with fear.

"Please, just let me get dressed?" My

throat is dry and my voice is hoarse as the words burn themselves from my chest.

"Soon, my little Peach. You see, your sister was in this exact same position once. When I sliced her, that smooth, soft skin bled for me." His evil words seep into my mind, and I shake my head so fast I feel dizzy. "Now, it's your turn."

LIAM

"What the fuck is taking so long?" As the sun rises, I pace back and forth, waiting for them to trace the location of the phone that sent the photo to Tayla. Her parents arrived late from their flight and walked in to the news that their daughter was taken.

"Liam, I know it's difficult, but you need to relax. They'll find her." Glancing at the warm, brown eyes of my girl's sister, I nod. She's so strong. I've never seen anyone with the calmness she possesses. I take her hand and tug her away from the police.

"Tay, I know I've been an asshole and there are things I've done that I am not proud of, but I need you to know that I care about her. I would do anything for her." She stares at me for a long while, and I can tell she's trying to figure out if I'm being honest.

With a small nod, she pulls me into a hug. "If you hurt her, Hayes, I will kick you in those jewels you're so proud of." Her words have me chuckling.

I wrap my arms around my sister-in-law and give her a squeeze. "Never. She's in my heart, Tayla. She really is."

We pull away, and she offers me a small smile. "I know, Liam."

"We've got it." A voice drags my attention from Tay. The officer who was working on a trace rises from his chair quickly, and we rush to him. There's a green dot on the screen flashing at the same beat as my heart.

"You found her?" I question and he nods, pulling on his gun holster and jacket.

"Ladies, please stay here. We don't know what we're dealing with or how volatile he is. You guys can come along." He points to me, my brother, and my best friend.

We head in the direction of an outhouse behind the main cellar I see in the distance. That's where my girl is? I'm about to rush toward it when Callum's hand holds me back.

"Don't rush in there like a crazy person. He may have a gun. Let the police handle it." I don't respond as we near the brick building. All this time, she was so close and I couldn't even find her.

The only sound is the crunch of our footfalls on the sand. She's in there, I can feel it in my gut. "Mr. Spencer, we know you're in there. Come out with your hands up, and we can make this easy for you." The deep rumble of the officer echoes around us.

We're met with silence, but my heart is kicking against my chest painfully and the sound deafens me. The thought of her in there cold, hungry, possibly even hurt burns through every rational thought I have. "Get out here, you fucking psycho!" My voice is loud and shrill, and suddenly I hear her.

The agony in her scream is torture to my soul. Shredding it, ripping me apart at the seams. Before I have time to react, the door is kicked in by one of the officers, and they rush inside.

The sight before me has my body

vibrating with anger and fear.

"Ah, now, all the men have come to save you. Look at that." His voice is sinister. Emma is caked in dirt and blood, and it's taking all my restraint not to run toward her.

"Please…" Her eyes meet mine, and I can see fear flickering like a flame in her gaze.

"Let her go, you piece of shit." The venom drips from my voice, and his chuckle sounds demented as he wields the blade close to her neck, setting me on edge. I'm about to pounce, but I know that will only hurt her so I swallow the acidic bile and wait.

"Drop your guns, officers, or the pretty little girl will get what's coming to her." The next few minutes feel like slow motion. I hear the crack of a gun, the sound of a bullet leaving its chamber, and my body goes rigid.

Her scream is loud, the sound rings in my ears. I'm frozen for a moment, watching the scene unfold. The man holding on to Emma drops to his knees, and the blade he was holding falls to the cement floor with a loud clink.

She's on her knees, and before I realize it, my feet are moving and I'm on the concrete with her. My arms encircle her and she feels small as she trembles in my arms.

Noise surrounds us, but everything sounds as if I'm in a tin can. My heartbeat is erratic, matching the beat of hers. Everything I've ever done in my life, all the shit that I've been through will never compare to the thought of almost losing her.

I lift her up, carrying her out of the building as her tears soak my shirt. I didn't even realize she was crying. It's as if I'm having an out-of-body experience. "Em, look at me, baby."

She does, but her reply is croaky and hoarse. "I... can't..." Her sobs are muffled, and her hands tangle in my shirt, fisting it, holding me to her. She's shivering, and the first thing I want to do is get her into a hot shower to wash the memories of the last few hours out of her mind.

"Sir, we're going to have to ask the lady a few questions."

I turn to find one officer behind us.

His comment stops me in my tracks. Her body trembles in my arms and a sense of possessiveness overtakes me. "Can we come to the station later? She's in no condition to answer anything right now." I glare at him. I know he's just doing his job, but I'm doing mine. Protecting what's mine.

"Yes, give us a call when you're ready." People are milling around, but I have one goal, and that's to get her back to our room where she can feel safe. We head upstairs with her parents and sister following. I set Emma down in the living room of our suite and lean in to whisper in her ear. "Did you want me to run you a bath?" She nods, while she leans in to Tayla's embrace.

Heading into the bathroom, I turn on the tap and pour her peach-scented bath oil into the steaming water. Staring at the water, I realize with certainty that I love her, that I don't want to live without her.

So much has happened to her over the last few hours, and I wasn't there to stop her from getting hurt. *Would I ever be able to protect her?* In my line of work, it's not easy.

We have stalkers and crazies that try stupid shit all the time.

Something dawns on me, and I wonder if he touched her. The thought boils my blood. If he did, she will need to go for tests first. Shit, I didn't even think about it.

EMMA

"I'm so sorry I didn't talk to you about what happened to me." My sister's big, blue eyes are shining with unshed tears. She feels as if this is her fault, but it's not.

"Tay, please, don't blame yourself." My voice is hoarse; it feels as if I've eaten sand.

"Babe, I should have told you. Explained." I glance up and find my mother and father standing behind Tayla. They're looking at me like I'm about to break, shatter like a glass ornament. "We can talk, when you're ready. I need to tell you everything." I nod, seeing the guilt on my sister's face.

"I would like that. I need to get cleaned up for the wedding."

She looks at me in surprise. "No, I'm cancelling."

"You're not! Please? Trust me." We stare at each other for a while and when she nods, I'm relieved. I want to spend time with my family, to be around people who love me. It's the only way I can get through this.

"Okay. We'll leave to get ready. See you downstairs." She pulls me into a hug.

Once everyone has left, I head into the bathroom.

"Liam…" My voice is tentative, and he stills. I watch him turn off the tap and face me.

"Peach…" The word effortlessly falls from his lips, and I can't stop the grimace. "Sorry, I… It's just… I mean…"

"No." My gaze settles on his as we stare at each other. "I like when you call me that. I just… it's too soon. I can't…"

"I understand. I do. Did he…?" He motions to my body and I know what he's asking.

Shaking my head, I murmur my response. "No, thank God, he did manage to slice into me but stopped when he heard you outside."

He steps closer and I lift my matted hair to show him my wounds. "We were too late." His words are barely audible.

"You were just in time, Liam. I asked everyone to give me a few hours to clean up. I want the wedding to go ahead." I peer up at him then and I can tell he's shocked.

"Baby, you've just been—"

"I want to do this. I can't let him win, and if I crawl into a corner and hide, that's what happens. I want you there, beside me. Liam?"

He stares at me for so long that I'm sure he's going to walk away. "Let me get the incense. I'll be back in a minute." He doesn't answer my question and as he passes me, I feel my heart splintering just a little more. I figured he wouldn't want a broken little girl. As the click of the bathroom door echoes, I stand alone looking at my reflection in the mirror.

Slipping the dress down my bruised body, I take in the purple and blue marks on my ribs. He made sure that I would remember him for days, even weeks after.

My body aches, but surprisingly, all I want are Liam's strong arms holding me, keeping me warm. The cold has seeped into my bones, and it feels as if I will never be warm again. The hot water has steamed up the room, and I tentatively step into the scented bath.

Sitting back, I feel the muscles in my body ease and the pain slowly subside. Heat envelopes me and calms my racing heart. *I'm safe.* Lowering into the water, it splashes over the cuts, burning them. Tears sting my eyes and I shut them tight, hoping for a reprieve from the memory, but it assaults me, leaving me a sobbing mess.

"The pretty little Emmy, isn't it funny how I watched you grow up, and here I am, about to take what I wanted." His fingers trace my spine. They're cold and calloused. Rough, like sandpaper. The blade moves over my skin, sending a wave of fear through me. "You see, your sister took your place. She took your punishment. Now that I found you, I intend to give you the same treatment she got."

"What did you do to her?" My whispered words fall on deaf ears as he continues his tirade.

"You made me want you. You acted like a little whore with that boyfriend of yours that your daddy didn't like. I tried to make enough money to take you away, but your daddy couldn't shut his mouth. So I got caught."

"What do you mean?"

"You're mine Emmy, all mine. I will mark you and wherever you go, whatever you do, you'll remember me. Just like your sister." That's when the burning starts as the blade slices into my skin.

"Emma, Em, baby?" A deep voice pulls me from the nightmare, and I glance into hazel eyes. They're filled with emotion—fear, anguish, love. My heart stutters as soon as I recognize it. *Love.*

"Liam?"

"You were screaming so loud, I could hear you in the living room." With strong arms, he pulls me up and out of the tub. Wrapping a towel around me, he lifts me in his arms and carries me to the bed. "Baby,

I shouldn't have left you alone. I'm sorry." His lips on my forehead feel warm, familiar.

"Promise me…" I stare into his eyes, hoping I am conveying my feelings with a look. I need him. I want him.

"Anything."

"Don't leave me again." Warm arms hold me and when I close my eyes, I calm. This is what I need, what I want.

"Baby, I don't want to, but I couldn't protect you." Whoever thought up that stupid saying—*sticks and stones may break my bones, but words will never harm me*—didn't know what it feels like to have someone you love tell you they want to leave you.

Pulling back, I tighten the towel wrapped around me and gaze into those caramel eyes that disarm me. "If you don't want to be here, then I suggest you leave. Now." Pushing up, I stalk over to my luggage, pulling out a dress that I wanted to wear to the reception dinner.

"Emma, please, I didn't mean it like—"

"Liam Hayes, I don't want you here because you obviously don't want to be here. So save me and you whatever fucking heartache that will come and walk out the door." Spinning on my heel, I head to the closet.

It's as if I can feel the frustration emanating from him. "Emma, I am not fucking leaving you. I meant that I feel like I failed you." His words have me turning to see pain etched so clearly on his face. He stalks to me, grabbing me with his strong hands, pinning me against the wall. "Do you understand how powerless I felt not being able to protect you? It's fucking with me. When the one person you fucking love is being hurt and everything is out of your fucking control." He's shouting now, but the only thing I took from his whole tirade was the word *love*.

"You love me?" Everything around us stills. We're staring at each other, but he doesn't answer me. Even though I know that's what he said, there's a part of me that doesn't believe it.

This isn't real. How can he love me?

He leans in, our mouths inches apart, his

hot breath fanning over my face. Cupping my cheeks in his big, strong hands, he grins. "Yes, I fucking love you. With my heart, mind, body, with every breath I take." The man before me, the man who makes my body come alive under his touch, his kiss, his heated, amber stare, loves me.

My heart gallops in my chest, every nerve in my body ignites with electricity, and a giggle tumbles from my mouth, skittering across the air between us. The soft sound of my laugh becomes a loud chuckle, which has my body shaking against his. Caramel eyes bore into me as his dark brows crease in confusion. "I fucking love you, too." The words fall effortlessly from my lips. His mouth crashes down on mine, and as scared as I should be about him pressing against me, I'm not. I know he won't hurt me. The kiss isn't hungry or demanding like our others, it's filled with loving. Like he's pouring all his feelings into me with his lips, filling me and leaving me overflowing with emotion so strong that my heart feels as if it's about to burst.

Placing my hands on his chest, pushing back, I stare at him. "Liam, I'm not ready for anything... I mean... I just want you to hold me."

"I'll do anything for you. Whatever you need, just tell me." His words warm my heart. He loves me. "Baby, you're incredibly beautiful, you're kind, caring, and you've changed me. You've made me want to have what Callum and Tayla have."

"Liam Hayes being romantic, never thought I'd see the day."

"There are times I will surprise you, and it seems today is one of many." He stares at me like he's trying to read my mind. We're new to love, to being in a relationship, but there's certainty in my heart that we've been woven together in fate's intricate pattern. One night turned into more, and I almost lost him. The cuts on my body burn, but they'll fade. It's the wounds in my mind that I have to work on. His eyes rake over me, and his expression hardens when he sees the bruises and scars. *A man who has been fractured by life's harsh reality now takes my broken pieces and mends them, making me whole.*

LIAM

Callum and I are at the end of the aisle. The police had just left after questioning Emma and confirmed that there's no chance that sick fuck will ever see the light of day again. She still chose me, and I am trying to come to terms with the fact that this beautiful woman wants me beside her.

"Liam, she loves you. Just remember that."

Nodding, I turn to face the doorway. The music stops and there's silence for a moment before a familiar tune starts. I recognize Lana del Rey, her song *Young & Beautiful* plays as my girl walks down the aisle.

She's got her long, chestnut waves loose down her back with a few strands pinned back. Her makeup is light, and her lips glisten. The dress she's wearing offsets her creamy skin. The bruises are hidden by a small shawl wrapped around her shoulders.

A shy smile that tugs on her mouth makes me ache to hold her. To show her how much I love her. No matter what the world throws our way, I want her. Nothing will stop me wanting her in my life.

Emma comes to a stop opposite me, and we all turn to see Tayla and her father. She's radiant. I sneak a glance at Callum. His eyes are filled with unshed tears. All my life, my brother has never cried. He's never let emotion get the better of him, but seeing him now I realize he's truly in love.

Dragging my gaze over to my girl, I find her staring at me. Cocking my head to the side, I give her a wink and the blush that pinks her cheeks makes me smile. She's incredibly strong, both sisters are, but something about Emma strikes me as resilient. I love her. I know I do.

"Take care of her." Mr. Quinn hands over his elder daughter's hand to my brother, and my heart fills with joy for him. I have always wanted to see him happy, to find true love, and now I am watching him get married, and I wonder if I will be allowed such a luxury. The thought has my gaze flitting back to the brown-haired beauty on the other side of the altar.

As the minister starts his sermon, I am distracted by her. By brown eyes and chestnut hair. By the smile that lights her face with the softness of an angel. The sweetness that I want to wake up to for the rest of my life. *Will I be able to give her a forever she deserves? Yes, I fucking can. I know I can be that man for her. Because she's that woman for me.*

The reception dinner is in full swing, and all I can think about is pulling Emma to the side and having a heartfelt conversation with her. Well, okay, not that heartfelt, more like pulling her off to our bedroom and showing her exactly how I feel about her.

I did say I would be worshipping her body, and I plan on doing just that, for hours.

The family is all here, my mother is chatting to Mr. Quinn, and I can only imagine they're talking about grandkids. Since Callum and Tayla are married now, I am sure the pressure is on to produce a few kids.

"Mr. Hayes, I think you're needed back in the kitchen." I glance up at the waitress and frown. She offers me a small smile, and I shrug.

"I don't go into the kitchen, darling." With a cocky wink, I turn to the dance floor.

"No, I mean, you need to go to the kitchen." I must have looked as confused as I felt because she pointed to the small door to the side of the building, and I caught a glimpse of a soft peach dress. Understanding dawned on me. My girl was playing a game, and what she didn't realize is that I love games.

Pushing up, I glance at the waitress and nod. Making my way to the open door, I find a dimly lit storeroom. Emma still wants me after what happened, and I want to make her forget, to make her only think of me.

When I push open the door, I find the

woman who's embedded herself in my heart. Who has effortlessly made me want to be a better man for her. To stop fucking around and focus solely on her pleasure. Her body and her heart.

"What are you doing in here, baby?" Her smile is downright devilish and mischievous, and I can't help chuckling. I know she's still scared; it flickers behind her eyes. The anger that raged through me at seeing her hurt is something I have never felt before, and I will be damned if that ever happens again.

"I wanted you to make me forget. After what happened, I want to feel you and only you. I know there will be more for me to work through mentally, but tonight, I need you, Liam." Her whisper is raspy and filled with need.

"I want to be there for you. You have no idea how much I want you right now, and if you're willing to let me show you how much I love you physically, it will be my pleasure, baby." Stalking toward her, I tug her into my arms. For a moment, I bask in her warmth, in her soft peach scent, and I know I can never let her go. Running my hands down the soft skin of her bare arms, I feel the goosebumps rise in the wake of my touch.

Big doe eyes peer up at me, and her lips quirk into a small smile. "Show me, Liam." My name on her lips sends a jolt of desire directly to my hardening dick.

"Are you absolutely sure, sweetheart? You don't have to do this. You know that right?"

She nods and cups my face in her delicate hands. "I want you." That's all I needed to hear. I leave her and head over to the door, making sure it's locked from the inside. With a quick glance around, I find exactly what I am looking for.

"Baby, I want you sticky, wet, and ready for me." I slowly unzip her bridesmaid dress, and as soon as it pools at her feet, I suck in a deep breath. Her lingerie is a soft cream color, and I can see her puckered nipples pushing against the material of her bra.

She's so fucking beautiful.

Kneeling at her feet, I gaze up at her and I can see the confusion, desire, and lust dancing in her warm, chocolate eyes. Hooking my fingers in the waistband of her panties, I slide them off. Once she steps out of them, I rise and so does my cock.

My hands grip her pert, sexy little ass, and I lift her up and place her on the freezer in the corner of the large storage room. "Take your bra off, too, baby and open your legs." She obeys, while she watches me intently.

"Liam, what are you doing?" Popping the cork of sparkling apple juice, I ignore her question and drizzle the golden liquid on her nipples. Time for dessert. I lick the wet trail of sweet juice, and her hands fist in my hair, tugging and twisting as she mewls and moans my name.

"Mmm fuck, you taste so good, so sweet, baby," I growl up at her as I work my way down her stomach. I flick my tongue over her belly button and slowly move to her bare little pussy.

"Please, oh God, Liam." Her moans are getting louder, but I don't care if anyone hears her at this point. I am overcome with lust for this woman. Drizzling more over her bare pussy, I place the bottle down and open her legs farther.

The sweet scent of her and the apples combined is like a drug shooting directly into my veins, alighting my body with desire I have never felt before. As I open her with my thumbs, I just about come in my slacks at the sight of her glistening for me.

Flicking my tongue over her honeyed center, I suck her clit into my mouth and bite down gently. Her hips buck and she rides my tongue as I slide it into her slick folds. Her eyes flutter closed, but I want her to look at me.

"Open those pretty, brown eyes, Peach. Watch me eat your sweet little cunt." My filthy words have her riding my face. Her hands grab my hair, holding me against her as she watches me eat her with lust shimmering in her glazed eyes.

Fuck, I need to be inside her.

"Fuck, oh fuck…" Her moans are becoming incoherent as I slide my tongue in and out, slow, torturous and when I feel her tighten, I bite down on her clit, and she unravels before me. It's a beautiful thing to watch as her body spasms and writhes and her sweet release drips into my mouth, and I drink like a man in need of sustenance.

As her body calms from the orgasm, I rise with my eyes glued to hers. The sated smile on her lips has my heart soaring. "Now you're going to get fucked, baby. It's going to be hard and it's going to be deep." Undoing my slacks, I push them down along with my boxer briefs.

Her eyes grow wide as I fist myself. "Please, Liam."

"Hold on to my neck baby, this is going to be quick." I lift her against me, her legs wrap around my waist, and I slide into her easily. Shuffling to the wall, I pin her against it, my hips rolling as I feel her warmth around my cock.

"Oh God…"

"That's me, baby," I murmur. My lips find hers in a scorching kiss while I plunge deep and hard into her, faster and faster. I know I won't last long, but I want her with me. My lips travel over her neck, tasting, suckling, biting. Her body undulates as her hips move with mine. It's an erotic dance, and our bodies move in rhythm with each other.

Taking. Giving. Relishing.

My hands grip her peachy ass. "This is mine, every part of you is mine. Do you understand me?" I thrust into her deeper, and she moans in response. The feel of her pussy pulsing around me sends me into overdrive. "Come for me, baby. Milk my cock, give me all your pleasure. Coat me in that sweet honey." Her body tenses, her hips bucking wildly as she comes apart in my arms.

It's enough to set me off, and my body goes rigid inside her, thickening and stretching her tight heat as I fill her with my own release.

EMMA

ONE MONTH LATER

"Grab this, Em." My sister is setting up the drum set for Liam. As I take hold of the cable she's handing me, she pushes up from the floor. It's been difficult to get back into the swing of things. When Cal and Tay got back from their honeymoon, the record label told the guys there would be another local tour, so here we are at the Hollywood Bowl.

I am still interning and about to be offered a permanent position, which means I can stay in LA and be close to my sister. We still haven't really spoken about what happened, but I know she will tell me when she's ready.

"Thanks." She grabs the cable and plugs

it in. Taking a seat at the drums, she pulls two of Liam's drumsticks out of the holder and taps each of the drums to make sure they're hooked up correctly. The sound echoes through the venue.

"Hey, Em," I turn to my brother-in-law and grin. He's dressed in a pair of ripped blue jeans and a T-shirt that reads, "Suck It" on the front.

"Cal, how are you?" He pulls me into a tight hug, and I reciprocate. They've all been so incredibly supportive since the incident in Napa, and I am slowly coming to terms with what happened. I have even been to a couple of therapy sessions.

"Good, I think Liam is looking for you. He's in his dressing room." Leaving the newlyweds, I head off to find my man. It's strange saying that. After all we've been through, he's been my rock, supporting me every step of the way.

As I reach the dressing room, I hear the sound of a guitar filtering through into the hallway. I knock and push open the door. "Liam?"

"Peach, come in." As I step inside, I take a quick look around. Since we arrived I have been helping Tay, so this is my first time backstage.

"Cal said you were looking for me." He nods.

"I wanted to spend some time with you before the show." I watch him place the guitar down, and he makes his way toward me. The spicy scent of his cologne envelops me as he nears. "I missed these lips." He leans in, planting a soft kiss on my mouth.

My body reacts and I arch into him, feeling his warmth. When his tongue traces the seam of my lips, I open willingly. The kiss is soft and sensual, not the normal devouring ones he gives me. My hands twine around his neck, and the scruff on his chin tickles me.

"I missed your lips on mine," I mumble into his mouth, which earns me a sexy growl. His arms wrap around my waist and he lifts me up, carrying me to the black leather sofa in the room. Laying me down, he covers my body with his. Rolling his hips, I feel how hard he is, which in turn causes a whimper from me.

I want this man all the time. It's an insatiable hunger that I can't ever satisfy. "I want inside this right here." His hand moves down, cupping my jean-clad pussy, and my hips undulate as I shamelessly grind myself against him.

"Yes, I need you." Tugging his shirt, he helps me pull it up and over his head. The toned, inked torso that greets me has me licking my lips. As he's about to pull my tank top off, a knock on the door startles us.

"Fuck off!" Liam's husky growl sends a shiver over me.

"Bro, we need you at sound check now."

With that, we hear the footfalls of Callum Hayes walking off, leaving us in the room of now-diminishing lust. My giggle echoes around us, and I'm seared by scorching caramel eyes.

"Fuck, this isn't over, Peach. I'll devour you after the show." Hastily, we head out toward the stage, and I find Tay and Kierra having coffee.

"Hey, Ki, I thought you were leaving?"

"After the show. There's something I need to fix back home." Her eyes are glistening with unshed tears.

"Fix?" She nods, but it's the look in her eyes that tells me this is something big.

"Yeah, I can't really go into too much detail about it."

"Does Ryan know you're leaving tonight?" The question falls from my lips, and her answering stare is evidence enough that she's guilty of not telling him.

"He won't care."

"Of course he will. You two have something special, everyone can see it." I glance at my sister who is nodding in agreement. The night of the wedding, Ryan and Kierra finally admitted their feelings for each other. According to everyone, it's been a long time coming. They're both stubborn and hot-headed, and I think this is going to make for one interesting conversation.

"Yeah, that's all it was, one night. There isn't room for more, Em. It's complicated."

"Look, Ki, everything in life is

complicated, but if you're not going to be honest with him, then how is he supposed to know?" My sister is right. They need to just lay it all out on the table, or it's never going to work.

"I know, you're right, but let me go home first. There's something going on with my parents, and if I drag Ryan into it, it's just going to complicate things more than they already are. I don't want him to get into a relationship with me when I don't even know what the hell I am doing."

"Girls." Ryan's voice cuts through our conversation, and I notice the look on Kierra's face. She's smitten with the man. If only she could stop her fears and trust in him. In his feelings.

That's what I learned with Liam. Once he let go of the fear, things worked out and now I see nothing but happiness when I look into those caramel eyes. It's a light that shines from him, one that I only ever see when he's on stage, but when he looks at me, I see it, too.

"What's up, Ryan?" Tay asks with a

small smile on her face.

"I need some help over on the set up, Tay." The fact that he's staring at Kierra while talking to my sister doesn't go unnoticed.

"Sure." My sister passes him, and his gaze flicks over me and Ki. Ryan is gorgeous in his own way—tall, built, and keeps a beard. The short, dark hair that seems to point in all directions always looks like he's just rolled out of bed. I would say he's about six foot easily.

"Are you looking forward to the show, Em?"

"Yeah, it's been a while since I've been to a show, so I hope you're bringing you're A-game." His deep chuckle reminds me of Liam. The two are similar in many ways—one of those ways being how much they care. Deep down, these so-called rock stars are just men who love their women fiercely.

"You know it. So stop distracting your boyfriend and let him play the drums," he retorts.

"I'll try, but you know when he's got his mind set on something, it's hard to get him to stop." My response earns me a chuckle. Suddenly the drums vibrate through the venue, and the sensation sends tingles through every inch of my body.

My gaze settles on the man who holds my heart in his hands. He's in his element with the sound check, and we watch as he plays their new release.

I am head over heels, and I don't want to be anywhere else but in his arms. Ryan leaves us and heads back to the stage. Cutting a glance to Ki, I notice her eyes glistening. She has these incredible teal-colored eyes. I've never seen anyone with the same shade before.

"Babe, you okay?"

"I will be. There's just a lot I need to think about. If I want to be with him, there are things from my past I need to sort out. So me going home will let me tie up loose ends."

"And when you get back, you're actually going to tell him? You're going to be honest about your feelings? Because let me tell you something, that man looks at you like you are his world, or rather, he looks at you like you make his world turn. That doesn't come around many times in life. So while you can, grab hold of it and don't let go." Her smile is sad, and she flicks her gaze at the man in question.

"I know, Em, there's just too much hanging over my head right now."

"I get that. Just don't let him wait too long." Pulling her in, we hug and for the first time I realize I'm getting to see the inner workings of one of the feistiest women I know.

"I won't."

"I know you two spent the night together at the wedding," I whisper, and she steps back. Her cheeks pinken and she laughs.

"Were we that obvious?"

"Yeah, you two lit up the room with the sparks flying between you."

"Ugh, I hate not being professional." Her nose scrunches, and I can see why Ryan is so in love with her. Beneath that fire is a sweet woman, and she's incredibly beautiful. Her hair is dark blonde, almost brown, her eyes are like a crystal lake that contrast against her tanned skin.

"You're the most professional woman I know. It's okay to be in love, you know." With that, we burst into a fit of giggles.

"You would know, since you've snagged the older Hayes brother." She gestures toward Liam. He's still in his zone, relaxed and happy. His smile sends tingles through me and my belly flips.

"I am, and let me tell you, Ki, don't let anyone take that away. You need to be happy. It's your life, not your family's."

She nods and her gaze settles on Ryan again, and I can't help smiling.

LIAM

Since we've been back, it's been incredible having Emma living with me. After the drama the weekend of the wedding, she's been incredibly shy, nervous, and even a little tentative when it comes to sex.

I want to give her space, so I've held her when she needed it, but it's been killing me not being inside her. Deep, hard, and rough. Swinging my legs over the bed, I head into the kitchen with the thoughts of her writhing below me running rampant in my mind.

Those beautiful chestnut waves, those dark eyes that glaze over with lust when she's turned on, and that body. Curves and smooth, creamy skin. Every inch of her is perfect. Sometimes I still wonder if she's really mine.

With my mug in hand, I head into the small room which I converted into a soundproof studio. It's been heaven-sent that I can work and not have to go to my brother's house to do it. Setting the coffee down, I grab my brushes. They're used to get different sounds from my drums, and I love playing around with new rhythms.

Pulling on my headphones, I start with the new song I wrote. It's going on the new album, and Callum wants me to sing it. For the first time in our ten-year span, I am going to be singing. It's always been my job to take the backseat, to let me brother do the talking, but he knows that this song means a lot to me.

I jump at the sudden feel of a hand on my shoulder. Spinning my stool around, I find big doe eyes peering down at me. "Baby." Pulling off the headphones, I offer her a smile. "I didn't want to wake you."

"It's okay. I woke up and you were gone." She's dressed in a skimpy tank top and a pair of Victoria's Secret panties that she told me are called Cheeksters, and God, her ass looks amazing in them.

"Come sit." I pull her onto my lap, and when she wiggles, my cock pulses. "Are you trying to get me hard, baby?"

"Maybe…" Her cheeky smile and those chocolate orbs are filled with wicked intention. Lifting her as I rise, I walk over to the sofa that I had put in here if I had Ryan or Callum over for work, and I lay her down.

"Close your eyes and don't move." She obeys and I glance around the room when an idea hits me like a freight train. Grabbing the guitar strap laying on the floor, I proceed in tying her hands above her head. Once it's attached to the steel arm of the sofa, I grab my brush and kneel next to her. "Keep those pretty eyes closed."

"Okay, but what are you—"

Her words are halted when I run the brush over her nipples. The material of the tank top is so flimsy that her buds harden into little peaks, and I can see them pushing against the cotton. The steel bristles of the brush run lightly over them again and again until she's whimpering.

"So beautiful," I whisper in her ear. Moving my hand lower, I run the tips of the cold steel over her stomach and down between her thighs. It's cold, and I see her shiver as goosebumps rise on her skin. When I reach the apex of her thighs, her legs fall open instinctively, and I tease her panty-clad pussy with the brush.

"Liam, oh fuck." Her hips rise up and her body arches.

"Do you want to feel it against your sweet lips, baby?" She nods and I drag her panties off. As they hit the floor, I find myself staring at her beautiful, bare pussy. It's glistening with arousal already, and I can't wait to taste her.

Bringing the bristles up her inner thighs, I alternate between left and right. An object that always creates intense beats on my drums now composes beautiful music with her body.

Her body undulates, and she's now writhing. As soon as it comes into contact with her core, she cries out. "Liam!" She's so fucking beautiful in the throes of ecstasy.

"Shhh, I am here, I will take care of your ache, Peach." I lift her tank top just above her beautiful, pert breasts and tease her nipples with the brush. They pucker and harden even more, and my mouth is watering with the need to taste them.

My cock is steel, aching to be inside her. Dropping the brush that will now forever hold a special place on my shelf, I lave at her nipples. Sucking them into my mouth, one by one, tweaking and tugging them until she's begging for release.

Planting kisses down her body until I reach her smooth mound, the scent of her arousal fills my nostrils, and I savor it. Flattening my tongue, I lap at her core. Her taste is my drug and I am addicted. I push her legs apart and glide my tongue along the slickness. Sweet, musky, and sexy. She's perfect. I glance up and find her staring at me, her teeth raking against her bottom lip as she bites down hard.

Our gazes are locked, and I see the fire in her eyes as I suck her clit into my mouth. "Fuck, Liam. Please just fuck me?" Sliding two fingers into her, I feel her walls cinch against me, pulling me into her. In and out, so slow, so agonizing that her hips rise trying to hasten my movements.

"You want my dick inside you, baby?" She nods. "Do you want me to fuck you hard and deep, making you coat my cock with your sweet essence?" Another swift nod. "Tell me, Peach."

"Liam, fuck me, please? Stop teasing and torturing me. Just fuck me." That's all I needed to hear. She's letting go, and I'm going to be there to make her fall and when she does, I'll be the one to catch her before she hits the ground.

Making quick work of my sweats, I fist my cock. He doesn't need any more encouragement because I'm holding steel. Kneeling between her smooth, creamy thighs, the crown of my cock nudges her. The heat emanating from her pussy has me groaning in satisfaction as I edge my way into her.

Her body opens for me, letting me in, devouring my cock. My hips move slowly until I'm fully seated inside her. "Open those eyes. Look at me." She does, and I find the exact emotion that I want when I look at her. Love.

"I love you, Liam Hayes." She smiles, and I follow suit. My hips move, back and forth as I make love to her. As much as my body is screaming at me to fuck her, I can't, I don't, because I want to love her.

"I love you, too, Emma Quinn." Her hips rise up and meet mine as our bodies move rhythmically in time. Our hearts beat in tune with each other, and when I look at her, I know my song is complete. She's mine.

EMMA

Rolling over, I find the bed next to me empty. There's a small note on the pillow, and on the front is my name, scrawled in Liam's messy handwriting. Grabbing it, I unfold it and smile.

Peach, I have a meeting at the record label. Be good. Will see you in a couple of hours. And if you're not good, take some photos and send them to me. -L

As I swing my legs over the bed, the doorbell alerts me that someone is here. Padding to the intercom, I press the button for the speaker. "Hello?"

"Em, it's me."

My sister isn't one to just drop by, she normally calls first. As soon as the door is unlocked, I push the remote and the gate eases open. Her new car is exquisite. A bright red little Mini Cooper with the black soft top. It fits her perfectly.

"Hey, sis," we hug, and I can feel the tension radiating off of her. "What's up?"

"The boys are at that meeting for the new contracts, and I wanted to take the chance to talk to you." Her eyes are so expressive, and as I look at them, I can tell exactly what this is about.

"Come in, let's get coffee. I just woke up." We head into the open-plan space, and Tay settles on one of the barstools. The coffee machine is state of the art and normally I would be hesitant to use it, but Liam bought me a smaller, easier-to-use one.

Getting the filter ready, I scoop two large spoons of the dark roast in and fill the water. Turning it on, I pivot to my sister. "Coffee will be a ready in a minute."

"Thanks. How are you doing?" She's apprehensive and I can understand why. We haven't really had a chance to talk about everything.

"Better. I have been to that shrink Kierra suggested, and she's been helping me."

"Good. I wanted to tell you… I mean it's been years, and I hid what happened to me from you to keep you safe. I suppose it was a bad idea." Her smile is sad, and her normally bright, blue eyes are dull. I hate seeing my sister upset.

"It's not your fault. You can't keep me safe forever, Tay. This is something that happened, and I need to deal with it. That guy, he was a psycho. He blamed Dad for how his life turned out. But he was the criminal."

"I know…" I turn and grab mugs. Pouring the freshly made coffee, I hand a mug to my sister.

"Let's sit on the terrace."

The bench seat is comfortable, and I sit cross-legged watching my older sister work up the courage to talk to me. To tell me what she went through.

"After you, Mom and Dad moved, I had a roommate at college. She told me about a job she had found where she was going to make enough money for her own apartment within a month or two, and since I was pretty much living paycheck to paycheck, I was intrigued."

She sips her coffee slowly and her big, blue eyes—now shimmering with unshed tears—stare out at the ocean. "But that's good, right?"

"Kind of, I mean, it was risqué." Her gaze snaps to mine, but I don't respond. All I can do is wait. "I had to dance. You remember that yoga I used to do?" I nod. "Well, they wanted me to do that, I wouldn't strip, just dance. Granted the outfits were questionable, but I had made enough to afford books for school, clothes, and soon enough a small apartment."

"Tay—"

"I was there for about three months, and then one night he walked in. I didn't recognize him at first. He had changed from what I could remember of seeing him a few times with Dad. He asked me to dinner and being naïve, I went." She lets out a small, wry laugh.

"It was only after a month that he told me who he was and when I threatened him, telling him I was going to the police, he got angry." Gulping the last of the coffee, her body shudders and I want her to stop. I can see her hurting, and it's killing me. "He told me he wanted you, but I convinced him to take me instead. To do what he wanted because I didn't want to see you hurt. He blamed Dad for getting caught and said that Dad had to pay."

It's then that my sister rises and places her cup on the table. When she lifts her top, I see that her whole back is filled with ink. I remember seeing glimpses of it in London, but she never showed me the full tattoo.

An angel wing on one side and the cherry blossoms on the other. It's breathtaking. "I love that, but what does that—" When she turns to the light and sits right in front of me, that's when I see it. A sob chokes me, and I can't speak. The tattoo blurs as my vision fills with tears, and as soon as I blink, they run down my cheeks.

"He did that." She inhales a deep breath

and continues. "One night he told me if I didn't listen and obey, he would find you. So I did. I laid on a table…" She goes quiet, and the only sound is of the waves crashing on the shore.

"I laid on the table and he did that." She turns to face me then, and I see her cheeks and nose are red from crying and her eyes are bloodshot. "I just didn't want him to hurt you." I pull her in and hold her as my sister cries in my arms.

My tears are streaming down my face, and I can't stop the sobs now. "Girls…?" Liam's deep timber interrupts the bonding session, and we pull away to find both Hayes brothers staring at us in shock.

"Baby, are you okay?" Callum is at his wife's side in a matter of seconds, and the way he looks at her makes me smile.

"Yeah, it was time to tell Em what happened, and I guess we got emotional." Liam stalks over to me, offering his hand. I slip mine into his and he pulls me against him.

"You okay, Peach?" I nod.

"Right, that's it. You girls deserve dinner. What do you say, bro? We can take them out tonight. Somewhere fancy."

"Sounds good to me. I'll call Ryan and see if he and Kierra want to join us."

The boys head inside and I glance at my sister. "Thank you, Tay. You've been a big sister that I can depend on, call on, and lean on all my life. And you're someone I look up to, always have. I love you, always."

"I love you, too, little sister."

EPILOGUE

"This is fucking infuriating." Turning to the front of the stage, I find my brother chuckling. "Callum, what the fuck did you do?" His shrug is enough to annoy the everliving shit out of me.

"Bro, seriously, I didn't do anything. I think the crew forgot to pack them. Tay is at home, she'll bring them through now." Since my sister-in-law found out she's pregnant, Callum has made her stay home and handle the PR instead of touring.

I know she hates it, but there's no arguing with my brother when he's got his mind made up. And now I am stuck with the fucking idiot doing my set up, and he's driving me up the fucking wall.

"Thank God we're close to home," I growl out, knowing my brother is enjoying my frustration. Ryan, on the other hand, is sitting and watching us like we're the most amusing television show.

"Liam, seriously dude, you're all strung up. Do you need to get laid? Is Em not putting out?"

"Fuck off, Ryan." I know he's joking, but sound check is in two hours, and I haven't even made sure my set up is ready. I always need to be ready in advance. Let's just say, I am a pain in the ass when it comes to my set.

"I plan to. As soon as this show is over, I'm going after her." My best friend's words rip me from my mood, and I turn to him in shock. Kierra left a month ago. We're still not sure what happened, but Ryan has been worried about her. We all have been, but she told us she'd be back.

My brother is pretty much a one-man show now that she's gone. Poor Tay has had to pick up the work, and I know my brother is a pain in the ass to work with.

"You going to finally tell her how you feel about her?" I question. Both Cal and I stare at him—he's made his decision. I can see it in his eyes. I know they would be perfect together.

"Yeah, it's time to bite the bullet. She's mine, it's obvious. I just hope she sees it that way, too, because I'm not sure what I'm going to do if she tells me to leave. Or if she tells me she doesn't love me." It's the first time in a long time I've seen my best friend so serious.

"Ryan, she feels the same, dude. It's written all over her face every time she looks at you. If I didn't believe that then I wouldn't be here telling you to go after her." My phone buzzing interrupts the moment, and when I glance at the screen, I can't help smiling. My girl is fucking naughty.

The photo has my body aching for her, but it'll have to wait until I get home tonight. Another message comes through, this one even naughtier than the last. Glancing up, I find both men staring at me. "What?"

"You're so fucking obvious. That Em?"

Blue eyes bore into me, and I nod.

"I'll be back." Turning, I make my way down to the dressing rooms, and as soon as the door is shut and the lock clicks, I flop onto the sofa and hit dial on her number.

"Hello…" Her whispery voice has my blood boiling.

"Peach, are you trying to give me heart failure?" Her giggle is sweet and sexy, which is why I am now sitting in my dressing room with the door locked and my hard cock in my hand.

"I was missing you. The house is quiet, and I was thinking about you."

"And what were you thinking, lying on my bed—our bed—with that sweet little pussy wet for me?" Her breathing stutters on the phone, and I hear the soft whimper. "Are your fingers on those sweet lips?"

"Yes, they are." Her breathy words shoot pure lust through me.

"Good, I want you to stroke yourself. Slowly. Then slide your fingers in deep. Imagine it's me, baby. Imagine my fingers sliding into your hot, tight cunt." My hand moves faster, stroking my cock. Fisting it as if it's her heat tightening around me. The thought of being inside her has me throbbing.

"Liam, I am so wet." A groan rumbles in my chest and my cock thickens.

"Jesus, Peach. I am rock fucking hard here. Finger your pussy for me, baby. I want to hear you moan for me." And moan she does. Her sounds fuel the fire raging through my body. Sparks shoot through me, and I can feel my release building.

"Oh... Liam…"

"Baby, when I get home, you're getting spanked for teasing me like this," I rasp as I listen to her mewl and whimper. "Then I am going to bend you over and eat that sweet, tight pussy until you're begging me to stop." Her breathing is ragged, and I know she's close. I want her to fly over the edge and soar into oblivion with me. "Then I am going to fuck you so hard and deep that you'll be aching for weeks."

"Liam, almost… I… "

My balls tighten in response, and I give her that final tiny push. "Be my filthy girl and imagine my cock buried deep inside your tight little ass while I finger your sweet pussy." Her orgasm grips her and me, because I am shooting my load all over my stomach listening to her come apart on the line.

Fuck, I would love to be buried in that peachy ass right about now.

"Oh God..." Her breathing subsides and she's quiet for a few minutes. My body shudders, still coming down from the orgasm.

"You okay there, baby?"

"Hurry home. I want round two." With that, she hangs up, leaving me gaping at her sassy mouth. When I get home, she's going to be eating her words, especially when she sees what I have planned for her.

LIAM

Stalking through the door, with adrenaline pumping through my veins, my plans for dessert with my girl have me rock hard. The house is quiet, and the lights are dim, just enough for me to see that she's not in the living room or the kitchen. Heading to the cupboard, I find what I'm looking for and make my way into the bedroom.

On my bed, I find the most beautiful woman I have ever seen. And she's all mine. Placing the items on the nightstand, I lean in and plant a soft kiss on her cheek. Trailing my lips over her exposed shoulder has a tremble rushing over her body, and a soft whimper falls from her lips causing my dick to throb.

"Wake up, baby." Her eyes flutter open,

and in the dark room, illuminated only by the full moon shimmering through the terrace door, I can see the mischievousness shining in her brown eyes.

"Liam, what time is it?"

"It's time for round two, cheeky little minx." Her melodic giggle echoes in the room, and as she rolls onto her back, my breathing hitches at the sight of her in my tank top and nothing else.

"See something you like, drummer boy?"

"Sweet Jesus, you're going to fucking kill me." Grabbing the silk rope that I normally use to tighten around the pouch I use for my drumsticks, I grip her wrists, tying them above her head.

"What are you doing?"

"I'm about to feast on your delicious body, inch by inch. Then when I'm done, I am going to fuck you so hard and so deep that you'll feel me for weeks after. Your body is going to be so full of me, you'll be molded for me forever." Tugging the top up over her head, I step back and take in the woman that's now completely naked on my bed. She holds every part of me, body, mind, heart, and soul.

"Liam…" Ignoring her, I grab the bottle that I retrieved from the kitchen. Uncapping it, I drizzle the clear, golden liquid over her nipples, watching them harden. The honey against her skin is luminous in the moonlight.

"Mmmm, that's my kind of dessert." Leaning in, I lave at her pebbled buds, raking my teeth over them, biting hard enough to send jolts of pleasure through her. "But I need something sweeter." Offering her a smirk, I grab the other bottle. With slow precision, the chocolate sauce decorates her smooth, creamy skin. Drawing a small heart on each of her breasts, I admire the artwork before adding a dollop of cream in the center.

"That's cold." Her laugh is infectious and I can't stop smiling.

"Good, now shhh. I'm having my dessert." My tongue darts out, tracing the line of the chocolate sauce. Once I have licked up the one, I suck on the sweet whipped cream. The sweet flavors, along with her own delectable taste, has my body aching with the need to possess her.

"Oh, God, Liam." Her moans turn to soft whimpering mewls, and my jeans are tighter than I could ever imagine. Grabbing the two tubes, one of dark chocolate sauce and the other sweet, clear honey, I drizzle a line all the way from between her beautiful tits to the bare mound of her pussy.

"Yes, Peach, I'll take care of you. Now open those incredible legs. Let me see your sweet, wet little pussy." Her legs splay, offering me a view of her beautiful body. Grabbing both ankles, I press feathery kisses up her legs. Her thighs are trembling, and I can smell her delectable arousal. Once I've tasted my way up her thighs, I ignore the spot where she needs me the most and trail my tongue up her smooth skin, licking the trail of sweetness away.

"Liam, fuck me. Please, I need you inside me." Her hips rise to meet mine, and I can feel her heat through my jeans. That's all I needed to hear. Pushing off the bed, my jeans and briefs find the floor in seconds, and when I'm kneeling between her thighs again, I offer her a smile before I grip both thighs, lift them over my shoulders and feast on her sweet pussy.

I lave and lick and nibble like a man who's been offered a buffet after being starved for years. Her intoxicating sweetness envelops me, and I find myself drunk on her. Insatiable. Needy. Addicted.

Her body tenses, tightening around my tongue. I glance up at her. Her body coming undone is the sexiest thing I have ever seen. "Liam!" Her cries are loud, and I'm glad I don't have neighbors close by because they'd think I was killing her with pleasure.

Her release slowly dissipates, and I can't wait any longer. I need to be inside her. Moving over her body, I nudge her entrance with the crown of my cock. Waiting for approval. Acceptance. When she lifts her hips to mine, I slide in effortlessly. Our bodies move as if we're molding to one another.

The erotic dance of us connected, one

person, one heart, and one soul overwhelms me. "I fucking love you, Emma Quinn." The words are strained and harsh, but the emotion I pour into the kiss as I swallow her moans shows her exactly how I feel. Her tongue tangles with mine, teasing and tumbling.

When I pull away, our eyes lock and she smiles. "I love you, too, Liam fucking Hayes." With that, I roll my hips, seating myself fully inside her body. Her legs lock around my hips and I fuck her, I make love to her, I bind her to me. Not just with my body but with my very heart and soul.

"Emma, marry me." The words fall from my mouth without a second thought. And as tears glisten in her eyes, she nods and just gives me one word.

"Yes."

PLAYLIST

Young And Beautiful – Lana Del Rey
When You're Gone – Avril Lavigne
Start Again – Red
Better Than Me – Hinder
Hurt So Good – Astrid S
Don't Let Me Down – The Chainsmokers, Daya
You Are Here – Denmark + Winter
Suffocating – Alyssa Reid
Cold Sweat – Band of Skulls
Ride - Chase Rice

Full playlist on Spotify

BONUS
EXCERPT

CALLUM
Backstage Series Book #1
(Callum & Tayla)

PROLOGUE

When you're the man every woman wants, the one that they would drop their panties for in a heartbeat. No questions asked. What do you do? I do what every other red blooded man does. I take advantage. But what happens when you find one woman that changes the way you feel about yourself. Your life. And your heart.

Do you recognize the moment your life changes? When you find clarity. When the constant confusion you have becomes an untangled ball of string. The notes that are caught in your head for days on end, suddenly play in an exquisitely constructed symphony.

That's what happened the day I laid eyes on her. When she slammed into me, spilling her milky cappuccino over my favorite white T-shirt. When chestnut eyes, and sleek ice-blond hair invaded my senses. Her sweet vanilla perfume engulfed my veins and all I could see was the delicate angel.

My name is Callum Hayes. I am a rock star, a rock god. The tabloids call me a bad boy. They write the articles I want them to write. The image I portray is one of sex and rock-and-roll. Isn't that what rock stars are meant to do?

I am sitting in my music room. The only place I can be myself. The real me that nobody else sees. Images that rush through my mind of what I crave to do to that gorgeous woman distract me from what I am supposed to do. Write.

The want I feel for her is primal. I ache to bend her over this fucking piano, pull her tight little panties down her toned legs and sink myself so deep inside that sexy little body, ruining her for any other man. I need her sweet cunt to mold to only my cock. To make her yearn and ache for my mouth on her, my fingers inside her and my cock claiming her.

Today was Tayla's second official day with us. She's got an ear for music and sound. So setting up drums and tuning the guitars is the task I set her today. Her role is to help out the *sound engineers on tour, and I can't wait to get her backstage.*

My mind has been filled with dirty images since her interview. I turn my attention to the notebook. The words are jumbled, like the muddle in my mind. She will be the death of me. If I can't have her, I don't know what I will do. Liam is right. I put myself in situations like this, but this feels different. The way her cheeky mouth challenges me, makes me wish to see how much I can challenge her.

There is one thing he is mistaken about though, that Tayla Quinn will be mine. Beneath me. Writhing. Moaning. Whimpering. Begging. When I take her and make her scream my name, she'll ache only for me. Callum fucking Hayes.

THANK YOU

Sitting here staring at the screen and I'm speechless. It's always daunting starting any journey, but when you have incredible support, and loving friends and an incredible husband, then it makes the hill just a little easier to climb.

I never know where to start with this, there are really so many people to thank, but I'll start at the top. To my drummer for putting up with my crazy ass. He's got to be crazy to keep me around, but I'm happy he does. Thank you for your never-ending support, for always being there when I'm feeling like giving up, and showing me support when I need it most. I love you.

To my BETA babes, I have no doubt that Liam wouldn't be where he is, (almost published), without you. Kenzie, Sel, Simmy, Jeanette, Heather, Lizzie, Emma, Christina, Lisa, Taylor. You ladies killed it with this man and I love you all. To my new BETAs, welcome to the ride, Danielle, Kate, Naomi, and Kristina.

And while we're here, the #sisterwives Kenzie (@mabkenyie_bibliophile) and Lisa (@bookgeek_readss) have laid claim to Liam.

To my amazing editor, Vanessa Bridges, you don't know how grateful I am to have found you. The time you took and the advice you gave have made this story shine, thank you a million times over to you and Tricia! I'm excited for the future books to come.

To my Dreamers, you ladies kick ass! You along with my Street Team, THANK YOU from the bottom of my crazy little heart. There are so many of you, but I need to thank Barb, Wendy S, Kathy, Shelly, Theresa, and Wendy.

To my crazy as hell IG smutty babes!! There's so many to mention, but I want you ALL to know I FLOVE each and every one of you #bookbabes!

To the authors I've met who support, repost, comment, share, like, and offer never-ending advice and friendship, THANK YOU.

A special thank you to two ladies who are incredible authors, and I may fangirl over them just a tad, they've shown me incredible friendship by offering advice and support. Who are there at the drop of a hat to answer questions, and never turn me away, K and M, you ladies KICK ASS!! When I'm all grown up I want to be like you. LOL!

BLOGGERS! I haven't forgotten about you in this long fucking ramble. EACH AND EVERY ONE OF YOU ARE AMAZING! Thank you for being the support we as authors need. You are appreciated and loved for all you do! #AllBlogsMatter #BloggersAreAmazing

Finally, to the readers. THANK YOU! For one clicking, and supporting me. I wouldn't be doing this if it weren't for you. Keep doing what you're doing by supporting indie authors, and leaving reviews. Share books you love.

Thank you for taking the time out to read Liam and Emma's story. Please let a short review on Amazon and Goodreads, it makes a huge difference in an authors life. ;)

Much Love xo

OTHER BOOKS

Stand Alones
Choosing the Hart
Love Beyond Words
Cuffed
Fragile Innocence
Perfectly Flawed
Black Light: Obsessed
Among Ash and Ember
Within Me (Limited Time)
Cursed in Love (collaboration with Cora Kenborn)
Beautifully Brutal (Cavalieri Della Morte)

Taboo Novellas
Sunshine and the Stalker (collaboration with K Webster)
His Temptation

Austin's Christmas Shortcake
Crime and Punishment (Newsletter Exclusive)
Malignus (Inferno World Novella)
Virulent (collaboration with Yolanda Olson)
Tempting Grayson

Sins of Seven Series
Kneel (Book #1)
Obey (Book #2)
Indulge (Book #3)
Ruthless (Book #4)
Bound (Book #5)
Envy (Book #6)
Vice (Book #7)

The Stolen Series
Stolen
Severed
TBC

Four Fathers Series
Kingston

Four Sons Series
Brock

Carina Press Novellas
Pierced Ink
Madd Ink

Broken Series
Broken by Desire
Shattered by Love

The Backstage Series
Callum
Liam
Ryan

Forbidden Series
From the Ashes - A Prequel
Crave (Book #1)
Covet (Book #2)

ABOUT DANI

Dani is a *USA Today* bestselling author of a variety of genres, from romantic suspense to dark erotic romance and even BDSM romance. She loves to delve into the raw, emotional journeys her characters venture on, and enjoys the dark, edgy, and sensual scenes that fill the pages of her books. Dani's stories are seductive with a deviant edge with feisty heroines and dominant alphas.

Dani lives in the beautiful city of Cape Town, and is a proud member of the Romance Writer's Organization of South Africa (ROSA) and the Romance Writers of America (RWA). She has a healthy addiction to reading, TV series, music, tattoos, chocolate, and ice cream.

www.danirene.com
info@danirene.com

www.ingramcontent.com/pod-product-compliance
Lightning Source LLC
Chambersburg PA
CBHW071305210626
46818CB00015B/2982